Books by **Ursula K. Le Guin**

NOVELS

Tehanu
Always Coming Home
The Eye of the Heron
The Beginning Place
Malafrena
Very Far Away from Anywhere Else
The Word for World Is Forest
The Dispossessed
The Lathe of Heaven
The Farthest Shore
The Tombs of Atuan
A Wizard of Earthsea
The Left Hand of Darkness
City of Illusions
Planet of Exile
Rocannon's World

SHORT STORIES

Searoad
Buffalo Gals
The Compass Rose
Orsinian Tales
The Wind's Twelve Quarters

FOR CHILDREN

Catwings Return · *Catwings*
Fire and Stone
A Visit from Dr. Katz
Leese Webster

POETRY AND CRITICISM

Going Out With Peacocks
Hard Words
Dancing at the Edge of the World
Wild Oats and Fireweed
The Language of the Night
Wild Angels

A Fisherman of the Inland Sea

Science Fiction Stories

Ursula K. Le Guin

HarperPrism
An Imprint of HarperPaperbacks

HarperPaperbacks   *A Division of* HarperCollins*Publishers*
            10 East 53rd Street, New York, N.Y. 10022

A hardcover edition of this book was published in 1994 by HarperPrism.

Interior illustrations by Michael Storrings
Cover illustration by Kirk Reinert

First mass market printing: September 1995

Printed in the United States of America

HarperPrism is an imprint of HarperPaperbacks. HarperPaperbacks, HarperPrism, and colophon are trademarks of HarperCollins*Publishers.*

❖ 10 9 8 7 6 5 4 3 2 1

ACKNOWLEDGMENTS

"Introduction," copyright © 1994 by Ursula K. Le Guin.

"The First Contact with the Gorgonids," copyright © 1991 by Ursula K. Le Guin; first appeared in *Omni*.

"Newton's Sleep," copyright © 1991 by Ursula K. Le Guin; first appeared in *Full Spectrum 3.*

"The Ascent of the North Face," copyright © 1983 by Ursula K. Le Guin; first appeared in *Isaac Asimov's Science Fiction Magazine*.

"The Rock That Changed Things," copyright © 1992 by Ursula K. Le Guin; first appeared in *Amazing*.

"The Kerastion," copyright © 1990 by Ursula K. Le Guin; first appeared in *Westercon 1990 Program Book*.

"The Shobies' Story," copyright © 1990 by Ursula K. Le Guin; first appeared in *Universe*.

"Dancing to Ganam," copyright © 1993 by Ursula K. Le Guin; first appeared in *Amazing*.

"Another Story" or "A Fisherman of the Inland Sea," copyright © 1994 by Ursula K. Le Guin; first appeared in *Tomorrow*.

Contents

A Fisherman
of the
Inland Sea

INTRODUCTION

ON NOT READING SCIENCE FICTION

People who don't read it, and even some of those who write it, like to assume or pretend that the ideas used in science fiction all rise from intimate familiarity with celestial mechanics and quantum theory, and are comprehensible only to readers who work for NASA and know how to program their VCR. This fantasy, while making the writers feel superior, gives the non-readers an excuse. I just don't understand it, they whimper, taking refuge in the deep, comfortable, anaerobic caves of technophobia. It is of no use to tell them that very few science fiction writers understand "it" either. We, too, generally find we have twenty minutes of *I Love Lucy* and half a wrestling match on our videocassettes when we meant to record *Masterpiece Theater*. Most of the scientific ideas in science fiction are totally accessible and indeed familiar to anybody who got through sixth grade, and in any case you aren't going to be tested on them at the end of the book. The stuff isn't disguised engineering lectures, after all. It isn't that invention of a mathematical Satan, "story problems." It's stories. It's fiction that plays with certain subjects for their inherent interest, beauty, relevance to the human condition.

Even in its ungainly and inaccurate name, the "science" modifies, is in the service of, the "fiction."

For example, the main "idea" in my book *The Left Hand of Darkness* isn't scientific and has nothing to do with technology. It's a bit of physiological imagination—a body change. For the people of the invented world Gethen, individual gender doesn't exist. They're sexually neuter most of the time, coming into heat once a month, sometimes as a male, sometimes as a female. A Getheian can both sire and bear children. Now, whether this invention strikes one as peculiar, or perverse, or fascinating, it certainly doesn't require a great scientific intellect to grasp it, or to follow its implications as they're played out in the novel.

Another element in the same book is the climate of the planet, which is deep in an ice age. A simple idea: It's cold; it's very cold; it's always cold. Ramifications, complexities, and resonance come with the detail of imagining.

The Left Hand of Darkness differs from a realistic novel only in asking the reader to accept, *pro tem,* certain limited and specific changes in narrative reality. Instead of being on Earth during an interglacial period among two-sexed people, (as in, say, *Pride and Prejudice,* or any realistic novel you like), we're on Gethen during a period of glaciation among androgynes. It's useful to remember that both worlds are imaginary.

Science-fictional changes of parameter, though they may be both playful and decorative, are essential to the book's nature and structure; whether they are pursued and explored chiefly for their own interest, or serve predominantly as metaphor or symbol, they're worked out and embodied novelistically in terms of the society and the characters' psychology, in description, action, emotion, implication, and imagery. The description in science fiction is likely to be somewhat "thicker," to use Clifford Geertz's term, than in realistic fiction, which calls on an assumed common experience. But the difficulty of understanding it is no greater than the difficulty of following any complex fiction. The world of Gethen is less familiar, but actually infinitely simpler, than the English social world of two hundred years ago which Jane Austen explored and embodied so vividly. Both worlds take some getting to know, since neither is one we can experience except in words, by reading about them. All fiction offers us a world we can't otherwise reach, whether because it's in the past, or in far or imaginary places, or describes experiences we haven't had, or leads us into minds different from our own. To some people this change of worlds, this unfamiliarity, is an insurmountable barrier; to others, an adventure and a pleasure.

People who don't read science fiction, but who have at least given it a fair shot, often say they've found it inhuman, elitist, and escapist. Since its characters, they say, are both conventionalized and extraordinary, all geniuses, space heroes, superhackers, androgynous aliens, it evades what ordinary people really have to deal with in life, and so fails an essential function of fiction. However remote Jane Austen's England is, the people in it are immediately relevant and revelatory—reading about them we learn about ourselves. Has science fiction anything to offer but escape from ourselves?

The cardboard-character syndrome was largely true of early science fiction, but for decades writers have been using the form to explore character and human relationships. I'm one of them. An imagined setting may be the most appropriate in which to work out certain traits and destinies. But it's also true that a great deal of contemporary fiction isn't a fiction of character. This end of the century isn't an age of individuality as the Elizabethan and the Victorian ages were. Our stories, realistic or otherwise, with their unreliable narrators, dissolving points of view, multiple perceptions and perspectives, often don't have depth of character as their central value. Science fiction, with its tremendous freedom of metaphor, has sent many writers far ahead in this exploration beyond the confines of individuality— Sherpas on the slopes of the postmodern.

As for elitism, the problem may be scientism: technological edge mistaken for moral superiority. The imperialism of high technocracy equals the old racist imperialism in its arrogance; to the technophile, people who aren't in the know/in the net, who don't have the right artifacts, don't count. They're proles, masses, faceless nonentities. Whether it's fiction or history, the story isn't about them. The story's about the kids with the really neat, really expensive toys. So "people" comes to be operationally defined as those who have access to an extremely elaborate fast-growth industrial technology. And "technology" itself is restricted to that type. I have heard a man say perfectly seriously that the Native Americans before the Conquest had no technology. As we know, kiln-fired pottery is a naturally occurring substance, baskets ripen in the summer, and Machu Picchu just grew there.

Limiting humanity to the producer-consumers of a complex industrial growth technology is a really weird idea, on a par with defining humanity as Greeks, or Chinese, or the upper-middle-class British. It leaves out a little too much.

All fiction, however, has to leave out most people. A fiction interested in complex technology may legitimately leave out the (shall we say) differently technologized, as a fiction about suburban adulteries may ignore the city poor, and a fiction centered on the male psyche may omit women. Such omission may, however, be read as a statement that advantage is superiority, or that the white middle class is the whole society, or that only men are worth writing about. Moral and political statements by omission are legitimated by the consciousness of making them, insofar as the writer's culture permits that consciousness. It comes down to a matter of taking responsibility. A denial of authorial responsibility, a willed unconsciousness, is elitist, and it does impoverish much of our fiction in every genre, including realism.

I don't accept the judgment that in using images and metaphors of other worlds, space travel, the future, imagined technologies, societies, or beings, science fiction escapes from having human relevance to our lives. Those images and metaphors used by a serious writer are images and metaphors of our lives, legitimately novelistic, symbolic ways of saying what cannot otherwise be said about us, our being and choices, here and now. What science fiction does is enlarge the here and now.

What do you find interesting? To some people only other people are interesting. Some people really don't care about trees or fish or stars or how engines work or why the sky is blue; they're exclusively human-centered, often with the encouragement of their religion; and they aren't going to like either science or science fiction. Like all the sciences except anthropology, psychology, and medicine, science fiction is not exclusively human-centered. It includes other beings, other aspects of being. It may be about relationships between people—the great subject of realist fiction—but it may be about the relationship between a person and something else, another kind of being, an idea, a machine, an experience, a society.

Finally, some people tell me that they avoid science fiction because it's depressing. This is quite understandable if they happened to hit a streak of post-holocaust cautionary tales or a bunch of trendies trying to outwhine each other, or overdosed on sleaze-metal-punk-virtual-noir Capitalist Realism. But the accusation often, I think, reflects some timidity or gloom in the reader's own mind: a distrust of change, a distrust of the imagination. A lot of people really do get scared and depressed if they have to think about anything they're not perfectly familiar with; they're afraid of losing control. If it isn't about things they know all about already they won't read it, if it's a different color they hate it, if it isn't McDonald's they won't eat at it. They don't want to know that the world existed before they were, is bigger than they are, and will go on without them. They do not like history. They do not like science fiction. May they eat at McDonald's and be happy in Heaven.

Now, having talked about why people dislike science fiction, I'll say why I like it. I like most kinds of fiction, mostly for the same qualities, none of which is specific to a single genre. But what I like in and about science fiction includes these particular virtues: vitality, largeness, and exactness of imagination; playfulness, variety, and strength of metaphor; freedom from conventional literary expectations and mannerism; moral seriousness; wit; pizzazz; and beauty.

Let me ride a moment on that last word. The beauty of a story may be intellectual, like the beauty of a mathematical proof or a crystalline structure; it may be aesthetic, the beauty of a well-made work; it may be human, emotional, moral; it is likely to be all three. Yet science fiction critics and reviewers still often treat the story as if it were a mere exposition of ideas, as if the intellectual "message" were all. This reductionism does a serious disservice to the sophisticated and powerful techniques and experiments of much contemporary science fiction. The writers are using language as postmodernists; the critics are decades behind, not even discussing the language, deaf to the implications of sounds, rhythms, recurrences, patterns—as if text were a mere vehicle for ideas, a kind of gelatin coating for the medicine. This is naive. And it totally misses what I love best in the best science fiction, its beauty.

ON THE STORIES IN THIS BOOK

I am certainly not going to talk about the beauty of my own stories. How about if I leave that to the critics and reviewers, and *I* talk about the ideas? Not the messages, though. There are no messages in these stories. They are not fortune cookies. They are stories.

The three last and longest ones are all based on the same gimmick: an absolutely, inexcusably implausible notion, not extrapolated from any existing technology, not justifiable by any current theory of physics. Pure hokum. Pure science fiction, as they say.

Writing my first science fiction novels, long ago, I realized that the galaxy was in some ways highly inconvenient. I accepted Einstein's proposition that nothing can go faster than light (not having any convincing proposal of my own to replace it with). But that means that it takes spaceships an impossibly long time to get from here to there.

Fortunately, if they can go as fast or nearly as fast as light, Father Albert also provides the paradox of time-dilation, which allows the person in the spaceship to experience a near-lightspeed journey as nearly instantaneous. If we're going to a world a hundred light-years from here at near lightspeed, we spend, according to our own perceptions, only a few minutes doing so and arrive only a few minutes older. But on the world we left and the world we come to, in those few minutes a hundred years are passing.

The paradox is a lovely one to try to handle in terms of the lives and relationships and feelings of the interstellar travelers, and I have used it in many

stories. But it messes up communications something
awful. We get to our diplomatic post a hundred light-
years away and have no idea whether the government that sent us still exists and whether they still
need that shipment of megathorium.

If we can't communicate, there can't really be
much interstellar trade or diplomacy or any other
relationship. And fiction's mostly about relationships, human or other. So I invented the ansible.
(Later on I gave the credit for it to Shevek of Anarres, who tried hard to explain to me how it worked;
but I invented it first.)

The ansible disobeys Einstein. Information is
immaterial and therefore (oh, I love science-fictional
therefores!) can be transmitted instantaneously by the
ansible. No time paradox, no time lapse. When we
travel the hundred light-years from X to Y, the history
of the past century on X is waiting for us on Y; we don't
have to wonder if the anarchosyndicalist utopians who
sent us have been replaced by a demented theocratic
dictatorship. In fact we can call them right up on the
ansible and find out. Hello? Comrade? No, sorry, this is
a demented theocratic dictator.

Though scientifically ridiculous, the ansible is
intuitionally satisfying, easy to accept and believe.
After all, in our world, knowledge and information,
even our living voices on the telephone, move (seemingly) instantly, as disembodied electronic impulses,
right round the world, while our slow, material bodies
can only walk or drive or fly heavily after.

Of course it is that (seemingly) that makes the
ansible work. But nobody has ever complained
about it. And now and then an ansible turns up in
somebody else's story. It's a convenience, like the
telephone, like toilet paper.

In an early story or two I said or implied that
unmanned spaceships could also travel instantaneously. This was a mistake, a violation of my own

rule that only the immaterial could go faster than light. I didn't do it again, and hoped nobody had noticed.

But in the mistake is the discovery; often it's the lapse, not the effort, that opens into the unexpected. Long after, thinking about those unmanned and illegitimate ships, I realized that the implication was that it's not materiality that makes the difference, but life or mind. The sole difference between a manned and an unmanned ship is living bodies, mind, or psyche. Oh, now, that's interesting. Which is it that keeps the manned ship from going faster than light—is it life, is it intelligence, is it intention? What if I invent a new technology that allows human beings to go faster than light? Then what?

As the new fake technolgy was as implausible as the ansible, and counter-intuitional as well, I didn't spend a whole lot of time fake-explaining it. I just named it: churten theory. As writers and wizards know, the name's the thing.

Having the name, I plunged into the experience, and spent quite a lot of time, good time, too, on the vocabulary. I needed words to demonstrate fictionally what instantaneous travel, transilience, might feel like, finding out in the process that what it feels like is the only explanation of how it works, and that where words in themselves are inadequate, syntax can take you straight to another world and home again in no time.

All three of the churten stories are also metafictions, stories about story. In "The Shobies' Story," transilience acts as a metaphor for narration, and narration as the chancy and unreliable but most effective means of constructing a shared reality. "Dancing to Ganam" continues with the theme of unreliable narration or differing witness, with a hi-tech hubristic hero at its eccentric center, and adds the lovely theory of entrainment to the churten stew. And finally, "Another Story"—one of my very few experiments with time travel—explores the possibility of two stories about the same person in the same time being completely different and completely true.

In this story I found churten theory apparently failing to find its technology, unable to get us reliably from X to Y without time lapse; but I expect they'll go on trying. We as a species do love to go very, very fast. My own attention in "Another Story" was lured by the marriage and sexual arrangements of the planet O, an intricate set of relationships and behaviors laden with infinite emotional possibilities. We as a species do love to make life very, very complicated.

I don't want to talk about "The First Contact with the Gorgonids," or "The Ascent of the North Face"—is anything deadlier than somebody explaining a joke? I am, however, fond of both. Funny stories, silly stories, are such a gift. You can't sit down to write one, you can't intend one; they're presents from the dark side of your soul.

"The Kerastion" is a workshop story. My assignment was for each of us to invent an artifact or a prescribed behavior or folkway; we made a list of all these items, and then each wrote a story using as many of them as we liked. Several oddments, such as necklaces of vauti-tuber, come from the list, as do the concepts of sculpting in sand and making flutes of human leather. My friend Roussel described her artifact thus: "The kerastion is a musical instrument that cannot be heard." A Borges story in ten words. I made a few hundred words out of it and enjoyed doing so, but did not really improve on it.

Of the stories in this volume, "Newton's Sleep" and "The Rock That Changed Things" are the ones I've had the most grief with. "The Rock" is a parable, and I don't really much like parables. Its anger makes it heavy. Yet I like its key image very much. I wish I could have given my blue-green stone a lighter setting.

As for "Newton's Sleep," the title is from Blake,

who prays that we be kept from "single vision and Newton's sleep." In the story it is further linked to Goya's extraordinary "The Sleep of Reason Engenders Monsters." "Newton's Sleep" can be, and has been, read as an anti-technological diatribe, a piece of Luddite ranting. It was not intended as such, but rather as a cautionary tale, a response to many stories and novels I had read over the years which (consciously or not—here is the problem of elitism again) depict people in spaceships and space stations as superior to those on earth. Masses of dummies stay down in the dirt and breed and die in squalor, and serve 'em right, while a few people who know how to program their VCRs live up in these superclean military worldlets provided with all mod con plus virtual-reality sex, and are the Future of Man. It struck me as one of the drearier futures.

The story, however, didn't stay with that, but with the character, Ike, who wandered into my mind with problems on his; a worried, troubled man: a truly rational man who denies the existence of the irrational, which is to say, a true believer who can't see how and why the true belief isn't working. Like Dalzul in "Dancing to Ganam," Ike is a tragic character, an admirable overreacher, but he's less resolute and more honest than Dalzul, and so suffers more. He is also an exile; almost all my heroes have been in one way or another exiles.

Some reviewers have dismissed Ike as a feeble strawdog, victim of my notorious bloodthirsty man-hating feminist spleen. Have it your way, fellows, if you like it. Fried spleen with backlash sauce? But however the reader may see Ike, I hope the story doesn't read as anti-space travel. I love both the idea and the reality of the exploration of space, and was only trying to make the whole idea less smugly antiseptic. I really do think we have to take our dirt with us wherever we go. We are dirt. We are Earth.

THE FIRST CONTACT WITH THE GORGONIDS

Mrs. Jerry Debree, the heroine of Grong Crossing, liked to look pretty. It was important to Jerry in his business contacts, of course, and also it made her feel more confident and kind of happy to know that her cellophane was recent and her eyelashes really well glued on and that the highlighter blush was bringing out her cheekbones like the nice girl at the counter had said. But it was beginning to be hard to feel fresh and look pretty as this desert kept getting hotter and hotter and redder and redder until it looked, really, almost like what she had always thought the Bad Place would look like, only not so many people. In fact none.

"Could we have passed it, do you think?" she ventured at last, and received without surprise the exasperation she had safety-valved from him: "How the fuck could we have *passed* it when we haven't *passed* one fucking *thing* except those fucking *bushes* for ninety miles? *Christ* you're dumb."

Jerry's language was a pity. And sometimes it made it so hard to talk to him. She had had the least little tiny sort of feeling, woman's intuition maybe, that the men that had told him how to get to Grong

Crossing were teasing him, having a little joke. He
had been talking so loud in the hotel bar about how
disappointed he had been with the Corroboree after
flying all the way out from Adelaide to see it. He
kept comparing it to the Indian dance they had seen
at Taos. Actually he had been very bored and rest-
less at Taos and they had had to leave in the middle
so he could have a drink and she never had got to
see the people with the masks come, but now he
talked about how they really knew how to put on a
native show in the U.S.A. He said a few scruffy abos
jumping around weren't going to give tourists from
the real world anything to write home about. The
Aussies ought to visit Disney World and find out
how to do the real thing, he said.

She agreed with that; she loved Disney World. It
was the only thing in Florida, where they had to live
now that Jerry was ACEO, that she liked much. One
of the Australian men at the bar had seen Disney-
land and agreed that it was amazing, or maybe he
meant amusing; what he said was amizing. He
seemed to be a nice man. Bruce, he said his name
was, and his friend's name was Bruce too. "Common sort of name here," he said, only he said nime,
but he meant name, she was quite sure. When Jerry
went on complaining about the Corroboree, the first
Bruce said, "Well, mite, you might go out to Grong
Crossing, if you really want to see the real thing—
right, Bruce?"

At first the other Bruce didn't seem to know
what he meant, and that was when her woman's
intuition woke up. But pretty soon both Bruces were
talking away about this place, Grong Crossing, way
out in "the bush," where they were certain to meet
real abos really living in the desert. "Near Alice
Springs," Jerry said knowledgeably, but it wasn't,
they said; it was still farther west from here. They
gave directions so precisely that it was clear they

knew what they were talking about. "Few hours' drive, that's all," Bruce said, "but y'see most tourists want to keep on the beaten path. This is a bit more on the inside track."

"Bang-up shows," said Bruce. "Nightly Corroborees."

"Hotel any better than this dump?" Jerry asked, and they laughed. No hotel, they explained. "It's like a safari, see—tents under the stars. Never rines," said Bruce.

"Marvelous food, though," Bruce said. "Fresh kangaroo chops. Kangaroo hunts daily, see. Witchetty grubs along with the drinks before dinner. Roughing it in luxury, I'd call it; right, Bruce?"

"Absolutely," said Bruce.

"Friendly, are they, these abos?" Jerry asked.

"Oh, salt of the earth. Treat you like kings. Think white men are sort of gods, y'know," Bruce said. Jerry nodded.

So Jerry wrote down all the directions, and here they were driving and driving in the old station wagon that was all there was to rent in the small town they'd been at for the Corroboree, and by now you only knew the road was a road because it was perfectly straight forever. Jerry had been in a good humor at first. "This'll be something to shove up that bastard Thiel's ass," he said. His friend Thiel was always going to places like Tibet and having wonderful adventures and showing videos of himself with yaks. Jerry had bought a very expensive camcorder for this trip, and now he said, "Going to shoot me some abos. Show that fucking Thiel and his musk-oxes!" But as the morning went on and the road went on and the desert went on—did they call it "the bush" because there was one little thorny bush once a mile or so?—he got hotter and hotter and redder and redder, just like the desert. And she began to feel depressed and like her mascara was caking.

She was wondering if after another forty miles

(four was her lucky number) she could say, "Maybe we ought to turn back?" for the first time, when he said, "There!"

There was something ahead, all right.

"There hasn't been any sign," she said, dubious. "They didn't say anything about a hill, did they?"

"Hell, that's no hill, that's a rock—what do they call it—some big fucking red rock—"

"Ayers Rock?" She had read the Welcome to Down Under flyer in the hotel in Adelaide while Jerry was at the plastics conference. "But that's in the middle of Australia, isn't it?"

"So where the fuck do you think we are? In the middle of Australia! What do you think this is, fucking East Germany?" He was shouting, and he speeded up. The terribly straight road shot them straight at the hill, or rock, or whatever it was. It *wasn't* Ayers Rock, she *knew* that, but there wasn't any use irritating Jerry, especially when he started shouting.

It was reddish, and shaped kind of like a huge VW bug, only lumpier; and there were certainly people all around it, and at first she was very glad to see them. Their utter isolation—they hadn't seen another car or farm or anything for two hours—had scared her. Then as they got closer she thought the people looked rather funny. Funnier than the ones at the Corroboree even. "I guess they're natives," she said aloud.

"What the shit did you expect, Frenchmen?" Jerry said, but he said it like a joke, and she laughed. But—"Oh! goodness!" she said involuntarily, getting her first clear sight of one of the natives.

"Big fellows, huh," he said. "Bushmen, they call 'em."

That didn't seem right, but she was still getting over the shock of seeing that tall, thin, black-and-white, weird person. It had been just standing looking at the car, only she couldn't see its eyes. Heavy brows and thick, hairy eyebrows hid them. Black, ropy hair hung over half its face and stuck out from behind its ears.

"Are they—are they painted?" she asked weakly.

"They always paint 'emselves up like that." His contempt for her ignorance was reassuring.

"They almost don't look human," she said, very softly so as not to hurt their feelings, if they spoke English, since Jerry had stopped the car and flung the doors open and was rummaging out the video camera.

"Hold this!"

She held it. Five or six of the tall black-and-white people had sort of turned their way, but they all seemed to be busy with something at the foot of the hill or rock or whatever it was. There were some things that might be tents. Nobody came to welcome them or anything, but she was actually just as glad they didn't.

"Hold this! Oh for Chrissake what did you do with the—All right, just give it here."

"Jerry, I wonder if we should ask them," she said.

"Ask who what?" he growled, having trouble with the cassette thing.

"The people here—if it's all right to photograph. Remember at Taos they said that when the—"

"For fuck sake you don't need fucking *permission* to photograph a bunch of *natives!* God! Did you ever *look* at the fucking *National Geographic?* Shit! *Permission!*"

It really wasn't any use when he started shouting. And the people didn't seem to be interested in what he was doing. Although it was quite hard to be sure what direction they were actually looking.

"Aren't you going to get out of the fucking *car?*"

"It's so hot," she said.

He didn't really mind it when she was afraid of

getting too hot or sunburned or anything, because
he liked being stronger and tougher. She probably
could even have said that she was afraid of the
natives, because he liked to be braver than her, too;
but sometimes he got angry when she was afraid,
like the time he made her eat that poisonous fish, or
a fish that might or might not be poisonous, in
Japan, because she said she was afraid to, and she
threw up and embarrassed everybody. So she just
sat in the car and kept the engine on and the air-
conditioning on, although the window on her side
was open.

Jerry had his camera up on his shoulder now
and was panning the scene—the faraway hot red
horizon, the queer rock-hill-thing with shiny places
in it like glass, the black, burned-looking ground
around it, and the people swarming all over. There
were forty or fifty of them at least. It only dawned
on her now that if they were wearing any clothes at
all, she didn't know which was clothes and which
was skin, because they were so strange-shaped, and
painted or colored all in stripes and spots of white
on black, not like zebras but more complicated,
more like skeleton suits but not exactly. And they
must be eight feet tall, but their arms were short,
almost like kangaroos'. And their hair was like black
ropes standing up all over their heads. It was embar-
rassing to look at people without clothes on, but you
couldn't really see anything like *that*. In fact she
couldn't tell, actually, if they were men or women.

They were all busy with their work or ceremony
or whatever it was. Some of them were handling
some things like big, thin, golden leaves, others
were doing something with cords or wires. They
didn't seem to be talking, but there was all the time
in the air a soft, drumming, droning, rising and
falling, deep sound, like cats purring or voices far
away.

Jerry started walking towards them.

"Be careful," she said faintly. He paid no attention, of course.

They paid no attention to him either, as far as she could see, and he kept filming, swinging the camera around. When he got right up close to a couple of them, they turned towards him. She couldn't see their eyes at all, but what happened was their *hair* sort of stood up and bent towards Jerry—each thick, black rope about a foot long moving around and bending down exactly as if it were peering at him. At that, her own hair tried to stand up, and the blast of the air conditioner ran like ice down her sweaty arms. She got out of the car and called his name.

He kept filming.

She went towards him as fast as she could on the cindery, stony soil in her high-heeled sandals.

"Jerry, come back. I think—"

"Shut up!" he yelled so savagely that she stopped short for a moment. But she could see the hair better now, and she could see that it did have eyes, and mouths too, with little red tongues darting out.

"Jerry, come back," she said. "They're not natives, they're Space Aliens. That's their saucer." She knew from the *Sun* that there had been sightings down here in Australia.

"Shut the fuck up," he said. "Hey, big fella, give me a little action, huh? Don't just stand there. Danceedancee, OK?" His eye was glued to the camera.

"Jerry," she said, her voice sticking in her throat, as one of the Space Aliens pointed with its little weak-looking arm and hand at the car. Jerry shoved the camera right up close to its head, and at that it put its hand over the lens. That made Jerry mad, of course, and he yelled, "Get the fuck off that!" And he actually looked at the Space Alien, not through the camera but face to face. "Oh, gee," he said.

And his hand went to his hip. He always carried a gun, because it was an American's right to bear arms and there were so many drug addicts these days. He had smuggled it through the airport inspection the way he knew how. Nobody was going to disarm *him*.

She saw perfectly clearly what happened. The Space Alien opened its eyes.

There were eyes under the dark, shaggy brows; they had been kept closed till now. Now they were open and looked once straight at Jerry, and he turned to stone. He just stood there, one hand on the camera and one reaching for his gun, motionless.

Several more Space Aliens had gathered round. They all had their eyes shut, except for the ones at the ends of their hair. Those glittered and shone, and the little red tongues flickered in and out, and the humming, droning sound was much louder. Many of the hair-snakes writhed to look at her. Her knees buckled and her heart thudded in her throat, but she had to get to Jerry.

She passed right between two huge Space Aliens and reached him and patted him—"Jerry, wake up!" she said. He was just like stone, paralyzed. "Oh," she said, and tears ran down her face, "Oh, what should I do, what can I do?" She looked around in despair at the tall, thin, black-and-white faces looming above her, white teeth showing, eyes tight shut, hairs staring and stirring and murmuring. The murmur was soft, almost like music, not angry, soothing. She watched two tall Space Aliens pick up Jerry quite gently, as if he were a tiny little boy—a stiff one—and carry him carefully to the car.

They poked him into the back seat lengthwise, but he didn't fit. She ran to help. She let down the back seat so there was room for him in the back. The Space Aliens arranged him and tucked the video camera in beside him, then straightened up, their hairs looking down at her with little twinkly eyes. They hummed softly, and pointed with their childish arms back down the road.

"Yes," she said. "Thank you. Good-bye!"

They hummed.

She got in and closed the window and turned the car around there on a wide place in the road—and there *was* a signpost, Grong Crossing, although she didn't see any crossroad.

She drove back, carefully at first because she was shaky, then faster and faster because she should get Jerry to the doctor, of course, but also because she loved driving on long straight roads very fast, like this. Jerry never let her drive except in town.

The paralysis was total and permanent, which would have been terrible, except that she could afford full-time, round-the-clock, first-class care for poor Jerry, because of the really good deals she made with the TV people and then with the rights people for the video. First it was shown all over the world as "Space Aliens Land in Australian Outback," but then it became part of real science and history as "Grong Crossing, South Australia: The First Contact With the Gorgonids." In the voice-over they told how it was her, Annie Laurie Debree, who had been the first human to talk with our friends from Outer Space, even before they sent the ambassadors to Canberra and Reykjavik. There was only one good shot of her on the film, and Jerry had been sort of shaking, and her highlighter was kind of streaked, but that was all right. She was the heroine.

NEWTON'S SLEEP

When the government of the Atlantic Union, which
had sponsored the SPES Society as a classified project,
fell in the Leap Year Coup, Maston and his men were
prepared; overnight the Society's assets, documents,
and members were spirited across the border into the
United States of America. After a brief regrouping,
they petitioned the Republic of California for settle-
ment land as a millenarian cult group and were per-
mitted to settle in the depopulated chemical marsh-
lands of the San Joaquin Valley. The dometown they
built there was a prototype of the Special Earth Satel-
lite itself, and livable enough that a few colonists
asked why go to the vast expense of wealth and work,
why not settle here? But the breakdown of the Calmex
treaty and the first invasions from the south, along
with a new epidemic of the fungal plague, proved yet
again that earth was not a viable option. Construction
crews shuttled back and forth four times a year for
four years. Seven years after the move to California,
ten last trips between the launchpad on earth and the
golden bubble hovering at the libration point carried
the colonists to Spes and safety. Only five weeks later,
the monitors in Spes reported that Ramirez' hordes

had overrun Bakersfield, destroying the launch tower, looting what little was left, burning the dome.

"A hairbreadth escape," Noah said to his father, Ike. Noah was eleven, and read a lot. He discovered each literary cliché for himself and used it with solemn pleasure.

"What I don't understand," said Esther, fifteen, "is why everybody else didn't do what we did." She pushed up her glasses, frowning at the display on the monitor screens. Corrective surgery had done little for her severe vision deficiencies, and, given her immune-system problems and allergic reactivities, eye transplant was out of the question; she could not even wear contact lenses. She wore glasses, like some slum kid. But a couple of years here in the absolutely pollution-free environment of Spes ought to clear up her problems, the doctors had assured Ike, to the point where she could pick out a pair of 20-20s from the organ-freeze. "Then you'll be my blue-eyed girl!" her father had joked to her, after the failure of the third operation, when she was thirteen. The important thing was that the defect was developmental, not genetically coded. "Even your genes are blue," Ike had told her. "Noah and I have the recessive for scoliosis, but you, my girl, are helically flawless. Noah'll have to find a mate in B or G Group, but you can pick from the whole colony—you're Unrestricted. There're only twelve other Unrestricteds in the lot of us."

"So I can be promiscuous," Esther had said, poker-faced under the bandages. "Long live Number Thirteen."

She stood now beside her brother; Ike had called them into the monitor center to see what had happened to Bakersfield Dome. Some of the women and children on Spes were inclined to be sentimental, "homesick" they said; he wanted his children to see what earth was and why they had left it. The AI, programmed to select for information of interest to the Colony, finished the Bakersfield report with a projection of Ramirez' conquests and then shifted to a Peruvian meteorological study of the Amazon Basin. Dunes and bald red plains filled the screen, while the voice-over, a running English translation by the AI, droned away. "Look at it," Esther said, peering, pushing her glasses up. "It's all *dead*. How come everybody isn't up here?"

"Money," her mother said.

"Because most people aren't willing to trust reason," Ike said. "The money, the means, are a secondary factor. For a hundred years anybody willing to look at the world rationally has been able to see what's happening: resource exhaustion, population explosion, the breakdown of government. But to act on a rational understanding, you have to trust reason. Most people would rather trust luck or God or one of the easy fixes. Reason's tough. It's tough to plan carefully, to wait years, to make hard choices, to raise money over and over, to keep a secret so it won't be co-opted or wrecked by greed or soft-mindedness. How many people can stick to a straight course in a disintegrating world? Reason's the compass that brought us through."

"Nobody else even tried?"

"Not that we know of."

"There were the Foys," Noah piped up. "I read about it. They put thousands of people into like organfreezes, whole people alive, and built all these cheap rockets and shot them off, and they were all supposed to get to some star in about a thousand years and wake up. And they didn't even know if the star had a planet."

"And their leader, the Reverend Keven Foy, would be there to welcome them to the Promised Land," Ike said. "Pie in the sky and you die. . . . Poor fishsticks! That's what people called them. I was about your age, I watched them on the news, climbing into those 'Foys.' Half of them already either

fungoids or RMV-positive. Carrying babies, singing.
That was not people trusting reason. That was people abandoning it in despair."

The holovid showed an immense dust storm
moving slowly, vaguely across the deserts of Amazonia.
It was a dull, dark red-grey-brown, dirt color.

"We're lucky," Esther said. "I guess."

"No," her father said. "Luck has nothing to do
with it. Nor are we a chosen people. We chose." Ike
was a soft-spoken man, but there was a harsh
tremor in his voice now that made both his children
glance at him and his wife look at him for a long
moment. Her eyes were a clear, light brown.

"And we sacrificed," she said.

He nodded.

He thought she was probably thinking of his
mother. Sarah Rose had qualified for one of the four
slots for specially qualified women past childbearing. But when Ike told her that he had got her in,
she had exploded—"Live in that awful little thing,
that ball bearing going around in nothing? No air,
no room?" He had tried to explain about the landscapes, but she had brushed it all aside. "Isaac, in
Chicago Dome, a mile across, I was claustrophobic!
Forget it. Take Susan, take the kids, leave me to
breathe smog, OK? You go. Send me postcards from
Mars." She died of RMV-3 less than three years later.
When Ike's sister called to say Sarah was dying, Ike
had already been decontaminated; to leave Bakersfield Dome would mean going through decontami-
nation again, as well as exposing himself to infec-
tion by this newest and worst form of the rapidly
mutating virus which had accounted so far for
about two billion human deaths, more than the
slowrad syndrome and almost as much as famine.
Ike did not go. Presently his sister's message came,
"Mother died Wednesday night, funeral 10 Friday."
He faxed, netted, vidded, but never got through, or

his sister would not accept his messages. It was an old ache now. They had chosen. They had sacrificed.

His children stood before him, the beautiful children for whom the sacrifice was made, the hope, the future. On earth now, it was the children who were sacrificed. To the past.

"We chose," he said, "we sacrificed, and we were spared." The word surprised him as he said it.

"Hey," Noah said, "come on, Es, it's fifteen, we'll miss the show." And they were off, the spindly boy and the chunky girl, out the door and across the Common.

The Roses lived in Vermont. Any of the landscapes would have suited Ike, but Susan said that Florida and Boulder were hokey and Urban would drive her up the wall. So their unit faced on Vermont Common. The Assembly Unit the kids were headed for had a white facade with a prim steeple, and the horizon projection was of sheltering, blue, forested hills. The light in Vermont Quadrant was just the right number of degrees off vertical, Susan said—"It's either late morning or early afternoon, there's always time to get things done." That was juggling a bit with reality, but not dangerously, Ike thought, and said nothing. Needing only three or four hours of sleep, he had always been a night person anyhow, and he liked the fact that he could count now on the nights being always the same length, instead of too short in summer.

"I'll tell you something," he said to Susan, following up on his thoughts about the children and on that long look she had given him.

"What's that?" she asked, watching the holovid, which showed the dust storm from the stratosphere, an ugly drifting blob with long tendrils.

"I don't like the monitors. I don't like to look down."

It cost him something to admit it, to say it aloud; but Susan only smiled and said, "I know."

He wanted a little more than that. Probably she

had not really understood what he meant. "Sometimes I wish we could turn it off," he said, and
laughed. "Not really. But—it's a lien, a tie, an umbili-
cus. I wish we could cut it. I wish they could start
fresh. Absolutely clean and clear. The kids, I mean."

She nodded. "It might be best," she said.

"Their kids will, anyhow . . . There's an interesting discussion going on now in E.D.Com." Ike was
an engineering physicist, handpicked by Maston as
Spes's chief specialist in Schoenfeldt AI; currently
the most hi-pri of his eight jobs was as leader of the
Environmental Design group for the second Spes
ship, now under construction in the Workbays.

"What about?"

"Al Levaitis proposed that we don't make any landscapes. He made quite a speech of it. He said it's a matter of honesty. Let's use each area honestly, let it find its
own aesthetic, instead of disguising it in any way. If
Spes is our world, let's accept it as such. The next generation—what will these pretenses of earth scenery mean
to them? A lot of us feel he has a real point."

"Sure he does," Susan said.

"Could you live with that? No expanse-illusion, no
horizon—no village church—Maybe no astroturf even,
just clean metal and ceramic—would you accept that?"

"Would you?"

"I think so. It would—simplify . . . And like Al
said, it would be honest. It would turn us from
clinging to the past, free us toward actuality and
the future. You know, it was such a long haul that
it's hard to remember that we made it—we're here.
And already building the next colony. When
there's a cluster of colonies at every optimum—or if
they decide to build the Big Ship and cut free of the
solar system—what relevance is anything about
earth going to have to those people? They'll be true
space dwellers. And that's the whole idea—that
freedom. I wouldn't mind a taste of it right now."

"Fair enough," his wife said. "I guess I'm a little afraid of oversimplifying."

"But that spire—what will it mean to spaceborn, spacebred people? Meaningless clutter. A dead past."

"I don't know what it means to me," she said. "It sure isn't my past." But the scan had caught Ike's attention—

"Look at that," he said. It was a graphic of the coastline of Peru in 1990 and in 2040, the overlay showing the extent of land loss. "Weather," Ike said. "Weather was the worst! Just to get free of that stupid, impossible unpredictability!"

A crumbling tower poked up from the waves, all that was left of Miraflores. The sea was rough, the sky low, dull, foggy. Ike looked from the holovid to the serene illusory New England and saw the true shelter that lay behind it, holding them safe, safe and free, in haven. The truth shall make you free, he thought and, putting his arm around his wife's shoulders, he said it aloud.

She hugged him back and said, "You're a dear," reducing the great statement to the merely personal, but it pleased him all the same. As he went off to the elevator bank he realized that he was happy—absolutely happy. The negative ions in the atmosphere would have something to do with that, he reminded himself. But it was more than just bodily. It was what man had sought so long and never found, never could find, on earth: a rational happiness. Down there, all they had ever had was life, liberty, and the pursuit. Now they didn't even have that. The Four Horsemen pursued them through the dust of a dying world. And once more that strange word came into his mind: spared. We have been spared.

In the third quarter of the second year of Spes, a school curriculum revision meeting was called. Ike attended

as a concerned parent, Susan as parent and part-time
teacher (nutrition was her hi-pri), and Esther because
teenagers were invited as part of the policy of non-
infantilization and her father wanted her to be there.
The Education Committee chairman, Dick Allardice,
gave a goals-and-achievements talk, and a few teachers
had reports and suggestions to make. Ike spoke briefly
about increasing AI instruction. It was all routine until
Sonny Wigtree got up. Sonny was a drawling, smiling
good ole boy from the CSA with four or five degrees
from good universities and a mind like a steel trap
lined with razors. "Ah'd lahk to know," he said, all soft
and self-deprecating, "whut y'all bin thankin about
goan oan teachin jollajy? Y'know? An lahk thet."

Ike was still mentally translating into his own
Connecticut dialect when Sam Henderson got up to
reply. Geology was one of Sam's subspecialties. "What
do you mean, Sonny," he said in his Ohio twang, "are
you proposing to take geology out of the curriculum?"

"Ah was jes askin whut y'all thought?"

Ike could translate that easily: Sonny had got
the key votes lined up and was about to make his
move. Sam, knowing the language, played along:
"Well, I personally think it's well worth discussing."

Alison Jones-Kurawa, who taught earth sciences
to the Level Threes, leaped up, and Ike expected the
predictable emotional defense—must not let the
children of Spes grow up ignorant of the Home
Planet, etc. But Alison argued rationally enough that
a scientific understanding limited to the composi-
tion and contents of Spes itself was dangerously
over-abstract. "If down the line we decide to ter-
raform the moon, for example, instead of building
the Big Ship—hadn't they better know what a rock
is?" Point taken, Ike thought, but still beside the
point, because the point was not the necessity of
geology in the curriculum, but the influence of
Sonny Wigtree, John Padopoulos, and John Kelly on

the Education Committee. The discourse concerned power, and the teachers didn't understand it; few women did. The outcome was as predictable as the discussion. The only unexpected thing was John Kelly's jumping Mo Orenstein. Mo argued that the earth was a laboratory for Spes and ought to be used as such, going off into a story of how his chemistry class had learned to identify a whole series of reactions by cooking a pebble, which he had brought from Mount Sinai as a souvenir and as a lab specimen—"following the principle of multiple purpose, you see, use plus sentiment—" at which point John Kelly broke in abruptly, "All right! The subject's geology, not ethnicity!" and while Mo was silent, taken aback by John's tone, Padopoulos made the motion.

"Mo seems to get under John Kelly's hide," Ike said as they went down A Corridor to the elevators.

"Oh, *shit*, Daddy," Esther said.

At sixteen, Esther had got a little more height, though she still hunched over as if her head was pulled forward by her effort to see through the thick glasses that kept sliding down her nose. Her temper was pretty moody. Ike couldn't seem to say much lately without her jumping him.

" 'Shit' isn't a statement that furthers discussion, Esther," he said mildly.

"What discussion?"

"The topic, as I understood it, was John Kelly's impatience with Mo, and what might motivate it."

"Oh, *shit*, Daddy!"

"Stop it, Esther," Susan said.

"Stop what?"

"If you know, as your tone implies you do, what was annoying John," Ike said, "would you share your knowledge with us?"

When you worked hard not to give in to irrational impulses, it was discouraging to get no response at all but emotionality. His perfectly fair request merely drove the girl into speechless fury. The thick glasses glared at him a moment. He could scarcely see her grey eyes through them. She stalked ahead and got into an elevator that seemed to open to accommodate her rage. She didn't hold the doors for them.

"So," Ike said tiredly, waiting for the next elevator to Vermont. "What was that all about?"

Susan shrugged a little.

"I don't understand this behavior. Why is she so hostile, so aggressive?"

It wasn't a new question, perhaps, but Susan didn't even make an effort to answer it. Her silence was almost hostile, and he resented it. "What does she think this kind of behavior gains her? What is it she wants?"

"Timmy Kelly calls you Kike Rose," Susan said. "So Esther told me. He calles her Kikey Rose at school. She said she liked 'Glasseyes' better."

"Oh," Ike said. "Oh—shit."

"Exactly."

They rode down to Vermont in silence.

Crossing the Common under the pseudostars he said, "I don't even understand where he learned the word."

"Who?"

"Timmy Kelly. He's Esther's age—a year younger. He grew up in the Colony just as she did. The Kellys joined the year after we did. My God! We can keep out every virus, every bacterium, every spore, but this—this gets in? How? How can it be?—I tell you, Susan, I think the monitors should be closed. Everything these children see and hear from earth is a lesson in violence, bigotry, supersition."

"He didn't need to listen to the monitors." Her tone was almost patronizingly patient.

"I worked with John at Moonshadow, close quarters, daily, for eight months," he said. "There was nothing, nothing of this sort."

"It's Pat more than John, actually," Susan said in

the same disagreeably dispassionate way. "Little sub-snubs on the Nutritional Planning Committee, for years. Little jokes. 'Would that be kosher—Susan?' Well. So. You live with it."

"Down below, yes, but here, in the Colony, in Spes—"

"Ike, Spes people are very conventional, conservative people, hadn't you noticed? Very elitist people. How could we be anything but?"

"Conservative? Conventional? What are you talking about?"

"Well, look at us! Power hierarchy, division of labor by gender, Cartesian values, totally mid-twentieth century! I'm not complaining, you know. I chose it too. I love feeling safe. I wanted the kids to be safe. But you pay for safety."

"I don't understand your attitude. We risked everything for Spes—because we're future-oriented. These are the people who chose to leave the past behind, to start fresh. To form a true human community and to do it right, to do it right, for once! These people are innovators, intellectually courageous, not a bunch of gutbrains sunk in their bigotries! Our average IQ is 165—"

"Ike, I know. I know the average IQ."

"The boy is rebelling," Ike said after a short silence. "Just as Esther is. Using the foulest language they know, trying to shock the adults. It's meaningless."

"And John Kelly tonight?"

"Look, Mo was going on and on. All that about his damned souvenir pebble—he plays cute a good deal, you know. The kids he teaches eat it up, but it gets pretty tiresome in committee. If John cut him off, he asked for it."

They were at the door of their unit. It looked like the door of a New England frame house, though it hissed open sideways when Ike touched the doorbell.

Esther had gone to her cube, of course. Lately

she spent as little time as possible with them in the livingcube. Noah and Jason had spread their diagrams, printouts, workbooks, a tri-di checkerboard all over the builtins and the floor, and sat in the middle of it eating prochips and chattering away. "Tom's sister says she saw her in the O.R.," Jason was saying. "Hi, Ike, hi, Susan. I don't know, you can't believe something some six-year-old says."

"Yeah, she's probably just imitating what Linda said, trying to get attention. Hi, Mom, hi, Dad. Hey, did you hear about this burned woman Linda Jones and Treese Gerlack say they saw?"

"What do you mean, a burned woman?"

"Over by school in C-1 Corridor. They were going along, going to some girls' meeting thing—"

"Dahncing clahss," Jason interjected, striking a pose somewhere between a dying swan and a vomiting twelve-year-old.

"—and they claim they saw this woman they'd never seen before, how about that? How could there be anybody in Spes they'd never even seen? And she was like burned all over, and sort of lurking along the side of the corridor like she was afraid of being seen. And they say she went down C-3 just before they got there, and when they did they couldn't see her. And she wasn't in any of the cubes along C-3. And then Tom Fort's little sister says she saw her in the O.R., Jason says, but she's probably just trying to get attention too."

"She said she had white eyes," Jason said, rolling his own blue ones. "Really gutwrenching."

"Did the girls report this to anybody?" Ike asked.

"Treese and Linda? I don't know," Noah said, losing interest. "So, are we going to get more hands-on time with the Schoenfeldt?"

"I requested it," Ike said. He was upset, disturbed. Esther's unjustifiable anger, Susan's lack of sympathy, and now Noah and Jason telling ghost stories, quoting hysterical little girls about white-eyed phantoms: it was discouraging.

He went into his studycube and got to work projecting designs for the second ship, following Levaitis's proposals. No fake scenery, no props; the curves and angles of the structure exposed. The structural elements were rationally beautiful in their necessity. Form follows function. Instead of an illusion like the Common, the major space in each quadrant would be just that, a big space; call it the quad, maybe. Ten meters high, two hundred across, the arches of the hull reaching across it magnificently. He sketched it out on the holo, viewed it from different angles, walked around it. . . . It was past three when he went to bed, excited and satisfied by his work. Susan was fast asleep. He lay by her inert warmth and looked back on the events of the evening; his mind was clearer in the dark. There was no anti-Semitism in Spes. Look how many of the colonists were Jews. He was going to count, but found that he didn't have to; the number seventeen was ready in his mind. It seemed less somehow than he had thought. He ran through the names and came out with seventeen. Not as many as it might have been, out of eight hundred, but a lot better than some other groups. There had been no problem recruiting people of Asiatic ancestry, in fact it seemed the reverse, but the lack of African-ancestry colonists had caused long and bitter struggles of conscience over policy, back in the Union. But there had been no way around the fact that in a closed community of only eight hundred, every single person must be fit, not only genetically, but intellectually. And after the breakdown of public schooling during the Refederation, blacks just didn't get the training. There had been few black applicants, even, and almost none of them had passed the rigorous tests. They had been wonderful people, of course, but that wasn't enough. Every adult on board had to be outstandingly

competent in several areas of expertise. There was no
time to train people who had, through no fault of their
own, been disadvantaged from the start. It came down
to what D.H. Maston, the "Father of Spes," called the
cold equations, from an old story he liked to tell. "No
dead weight on board!" was the moral of the story.
"Too many lives depend on every choice we make! If
we could afford to be sentimental—if we could take the
easy way—nobody would rejoice more sincerely than I.
But we can have only one criterion: excellence. Physical and mental excellence in every respect. Any appli-
cant who meets that criterion is in. Any one who
doesn't, is out."

So even in the Union days there had only been
three blacks in the Society. The genius mathemati-
cian Madison Aless had tragically developed slowrad symptoms, and after his suicide the Vezys, a brilliant young couple from England, had dropped out
and gone home; a loss not only to ethnicity but to
multinationality in Spes, for it left only a handful
from countries other than the Union and the U.S.A.
But, as Maston had pointed out, that meant nothing,
because the concept of nationality meant nothing,
while the concept of community meant everything.

David Henry Maston had applied the cold equations to himself. Sixty-one when the Colony moved to
California, he had stayed behind in the States. "By the
time Spes is built," he had said, "I'll be seventy. A
seventy-year-old man take up the place a working
scientist, a breeding woman, a 200-IQ kid could fill?
Don't make jokes!" Maston was still alive, down there.
Now and then he came in on the Network from
Indianapolis with some advice, always masterful,
imperative, though sometimes, these days, a bit off
the mark.

But why was Ike lying here thinking about old
Maston? His train of thought trailed off into the
incoherencies of advancing sleep. Just as he

relaxed, a thrill of terror jolted through him stiff-
ening every muscle for a moment—the old fear
from far, far back, the fear of being helpless, mind-
less, the fear of sleep itself. Then that too was
gone. Ike Rose was gone. A warm body sighed in
the darkness inside the little bright object bal-
anced elegantly in the orbit of the moon.

Linda Jones and Treese Gerlack were twelve. When
Esther stopped them to ask questions they were partly
shy with her, and partly rude, because even if she
was sixteen, she was really gutwrenching-looking
with those glass things she wore, and Timmy Kelly
called her Kikey, and Timmy Kelly was so incredibly
gorge. So Linda sort of looked away and acted like
she didn't hear her, but Treese was kind of flattered,
actually. She laughed and said yeah they really had
absolutely seen this gutwrenching woman and she
was really like burned all over, shiny, even her
clothes burned off except sort of a rag thing. "Her
breasts were just hanging there and they were really
weird, really long," Treese said, "they were really gut,
right? Hanging down. God!"

"Did she have white eyes?"

"You mean like Punky Fort said she saw? I don't
know. We weren't all that close."

"It was her teeth were white," Linda said,
unable to let Treese do all the describing. "They
were all white, like a skull would be, right, and like
she had too many teeth."

"Like in those history vids," Treese said, "you
know, all those people that used to live where that
was before the desert, right, Africa? That's what she
looked like. Like those famine people. Do you think
there was some accident they didn't tell us about?
Maybe EVA? And she got like fried, and went crazy,
and she's hiding now."

They weren't stupid, Treese and Linda, not at all—no doubt IQs over 150 like everybody else—but they'd been born in the Colony. They'd never lived outside.

Esther had. She remembered. The Roses had joined when she was seven. She remembered all sorts of stuff about the city where they had lived before they joined, Philadelphia; stuff like cockroaches, rain, pollution alerts, and her best friend in the building, Saviora, who had ten million little tiny short braids each one tied with a red thread and a blue bead. Her best friend in the building and in the Building Mothers' School and in the world. Until she had to go live in the United States and then Bakersfield and be decontaminated, decontaminated of everything, the germs and viruses and funguses, the roaches and the radiation and the rain, the red threads and the blue beads and the bright eyes. "Hey I'll see for you, ole blindy-eyes," Saviora had said when Esther had the first operation and it didn't help. "I just be your eyes, OK? And you be my brain, OK, in arithmetic?"

It was weird how she could remember that, nearly ten years ago. She could hear Saviora's voice, the way she sang the word "arithmetic," with a fall and rise in it so it sounded like something foreign, incomprehensible, marvelous, blue and red. . . .

"Arith-metic," she said aloud, going down BB Corridor, but she could not say it right.

All right, so maybe this burned woman was a black woman. But that didn't explain how she got into 2-C, or the O.R., or onto the Plaza in Florida, where a girl called Oona Chang and her little brother claimed to have seen her last night just after sun-out.

Oh, shit, I just wish I could see, Esther Rose thought as she walked across the Common, which to her was a blue-green blur. What's the use? That woman could be walking in front of me right now and I wouldn't even know it, I'd think it was just somebody that belonged. Anyhow how could there be a stowaway? After a year and a half in space? Where's she been till now? And there hasn't been any accident. It's just kids. Playing ghosts, trying to scare each other and getting scared. Getting scared of those old history vids, those black faces, grinning with famine, when all the faces in your whole world were soft and white and fat.

"The Sleep of Reason engenders monsters," Esther Rose said aloud. She had pored over the Monuments of Western Art file in the library because even though she couldn't see the world, or even Spes, she could see pictures if they were close enough. Engravings were the best, they didn't go all to blobs of color when she enlarged them on the screen, but kept making sense, the strong black lines, the shadows and highlights that built up the forms. Goya, it was. The bat things coming out of the man's head while he slept at a table full of books, and down below were the words that meant "The Sleep of Reason engenders monsters" in English, the only language she would ever know. Roaches, rain, Spanish, all washed away. Of course Spanish was in the AI. Everything was. You could learn Spanish if you wanted to. But what use could it possibly be, when the AI could translate it into English faster than you could read or think? What use would there be knowing some language that nobody spoke but you?

When she got home she was going to ask Susan about going to live in the A-Ed dorm in Boulder. She would do it. Today. When she got home. She had to get out. The dorm couldn't be worse than home. Their incredible family, Daddy and Mommy and Bubby and Sis, like something from the nineteens! The womb within the womb! And here's Uterine Rose, Space Heroine, groping home across the plastic grass. . . . She got there and hissed the door open and, seeing her mother working on her little kitchen computer, faced her heroically and said, "Susan, I want to go live at the dorms. I just think it would be a lot better. Is that going to make Ike go nova?"

The silence was long enough that she came closer to her mother and made out that she seemed to be crying.

"Oh," she said, "oh, I didn't—"

"It's OK. It isn't you, honey. It's Eddie."

Her mother's half brother was the only relative she had left. They kept in touch through the Network outlinks. Not often, because Ike was so strongly against keeping up personal communication with people down below, and Susan didn't like doing things she couldn't tell him she was doing. But she had told Esther, and Esther had treasured her mother's trust.

"Is he sick?" she asked, feeling sick.

"He died. Real fast. One of the RMVs. Bella sent word."

Susan spoke softly and quite naturally. Esther stood there a while, then went and touched her mother's shoulder timidly. Susan turned to her, embraced her, holding on to her, and began to weep aloud and talk. "Oh, Esther, he was so good, he was so good, he was so good! We always stuck it out together, all the stepmothers and the girlfriends and the awful places we had to live, it was always OK because of Eddie, he made it OK. He was my family, Esther. He was my family!"

Maybe the word did mean something.

Her mother quieted down and let her go. "Do you have to not tell Ike?" Esther asked, while she made them some tea.

Susan shook her head. "I don't care if he knows I talked with Eddie, now. But Bella just put a letter into the Net. We didn't talk."

Esther gave her her tea; she sipped it and sighed.

"You want to live in the A-Ed dorms," she said.

Esther nodded, feeling guilty about talking about it, about deserting her mother. "I guess. I don't know."

"I think it's a good idea. Try it out, anyhow."

"You do? . . . But will he, you know, get all . . . you know."

"Yes," Susan said. "But, so?"

"I guess I really want to."

"So, apply."

"Does he have to approve the application?"

"No. You're sixteen. Age of reason. Society Code says so."

"I don't always feel so reasonable."

"You'll do. A fair imitation."

"It's when he gets so, you know, like he has to control everything or everything will be out of control, I get sort of out of control."

"I know. But he can handle this. He'll be proud of you for going to A-Ed early. Just let him blow off a while, he'll calm down."

Ike surprised them. He did not blow up or blow off. He met Esther's demand calmly. "Sure," he said. "After your eye transplant."

"After—?"

"You don't intend to start your adult life with a severe, curable handicap. That would be stupid, Esther. You want your independence. So you need physical independence. First get your eyes—then fly. You thought I'd try to hold you back? Daughter, I want to see you flying!"

"But—"

He waited.

"Is she ready?" Susan asked. "Have the doctors said something I hadn't heard?"

"Thirty days of immune-system prep, and she can receive a double eye transplant. I talked to Dick

after Health Board yesterday. She can go over and
choose a pair tomorrow."

"Choose eyes?" Noah said. "Gutwrenching!"

"What if I, what if I don't want to," Esther said.

"Don't want to? Don't want to see?"

She did not look at either of them. Her mother
was silent.

"You would be giving in to fear, which is natural,
but unworthy of you. And so you would merely
cheat yourself out of so many weeks or months of
perfect vision."

"But it says I'm at the age of reason. So I can
make my own choices."

"Of course you can, and will. You'll make the
reasonable choice. I have confidence in you, daughter. Show me that it's justified."

Immune-system prep was nearly as bad as decon-
tamination. Some days she couldn't pay attention to
anything but the tubes and machines. Other days
she felt human enough to get bored and be glad
when Noah came to the Health Center to see her.
"Hey," he said, "did you hear about the Hag? All
kinds of people over in Urban have seen her. It started
with this baby getting excited, and then its mother
saw her, and then a whole bunch of people did.
She's supposed to be real small and old and she's
sort of Asian, you know, with those eyes like Yukio
and Fred have, but she's all bent over and her legs
are weird. And she goes around picking up stuff off
the deck, like it was litter, only nothing's there, and
she puts it in this bag she has. And when they walk
towards her she just goes out of sight. And she has
this real gut mouth without any teeth in it."

"Is the burned woman still around?"

"Well, some women in Florida were having
some committee meeting and all of a sudden there

were these other people sitting at the table and they were black. And they all looked at them and they just like went out of sight."

"Wow," Esther said.

"Dad got himself on this Emergency Committee with mostly psychologists, and they have it all worked out about mass hallucination and environmental deprivation and like that. He'll tell you all about it."

"Yeah, he will."

"Hey Es."

"Hey No."

"Are they, I mean. Is it. Do they."

"Yeah," she said. "First they take out the old ones. Then they put in the new ones. Then they do the wiring."

"Wow."

"Yeah."

"Did you really have to like, go and choose . . . "

"No. The meds pick out whatever's most compatible genetically. They got some nice Jewish eyes for me."

"Honest?"

"I was kidding. Maybe."

"It'll be great if you can see really well," Noah said, and she heard in his voice for the first time the huskiness like a double-reed instrument, oboe or bassoon, the first breaking.

"Hey, have you got your *Satyagraha* tape, I want to hear that," she said. They shared a passion for twentieth-century opera.

"It has no intellectual complexity," Noah said in Ike's intonation. "I find an absence of thought."

"Yeah," said Esther, "and it's all in Sanskrit."

Noah put on the last act. They listened to the tenor singing ascending scales in Sanskrit. Esther closed her eyes. The high, pure voice went up and up, like mountain peaks above the mists.

*   *   *

"We can be optimistic," the doctor said.

"What do you mean?" Susan said.

"They can't guarantee, Sue," Ike said.

"Why not? This was presented as a routine procedure!"

"In an ordinary case—"

"Are there ordinary cases?"

"Yes," the doctor said. "And this one is extraordinary. The operation was absolutely trouble free. So was the IS prep. However, her current reaction raises the possibility—a low probability but a possibility—of partial or total rejection."

"Blindness."

"Sue, you know that even if she rejects these implants, they can try again."

"Electronic implants might in fact be the better course. They'll preserve optical function and give spatial orientation. And there are sonar headbands for periods of visual nonfunction."

"So we can be optimistic," Susan said.

"Guardedly," said the doctor.

"I let you do this," Susan said. "I let you do this, and I could have stopped you." She turned away from him and went down the corridor.

He was due at the Bays, overdue in fact, but he walked across Urban to the farther elevator bank instead of dropping straight down from the Health Center. He needed a moment to be alone and think. This whole thing about Esther's operation was hard to handle, on top of the mass hysteria phenomena, and now if Susan was going to let him down . . . He kept feeling a driving, aching need to be alone. Not to sit with Esther, not to talk to doctors, not to reason with Susan, not to go to committee meetings, not to listen to hysterics reporting their hallucinations—just to be alone, sitting at his Schoenfeldt screen, in the night, in peace.

"Look at that," said a tall man, Laxness of EVAC, stopping beside Ike in Urban Square and staring. "What next? What do you think is really going on, Rose?"

Ike followed Laxness's gaze. He saw the high brick and stone facades of Urban and a boy crossing the street-corridor.

"The kid?"

"Yes. My God. Look at them."

The kid was gone, but Laxness kept staring, and swallowed as if he felt sick.

"He's gone, Morten."

"They must be from some famine," Laxness said, his gaze unwavering. "You know, the first couple of times, I thought they were holovid projections. I thought somebody had to be doing this to us. Somebody with a screw loose in Communications or something."

"We've investigated that possibility," Ike said.

"Look at their arms. Jesus!"

"There's nothing there, Morten."

Laxness looked at him. "Are you blind?"

"There is nothing there."

Laxness stared at him as if he were the hallucination. "What I think it is, is our guilt," he said, looking back at whatever it was he saw across the Square. "But what are we supposed to do? I don't understand." He started forward suddenly, striding with purpose, and then stopped and looked around with the distressed, embarrassed expression Ike was getting used to seeing on people's faces when their hallucinations popped.

Ike came on past him. He wanted to say something to Laxness, but did not know what to say.

As he entered the streetlike corridor he had a curious sensation of pushing into and through a substance, or substances or presences, crowded thickly, not impeding him, not palpable, only many non-touches like very slight electric shocks on his arms and shoulders, breaths across his face, an intangible resistance. He walked ahead, came to the elevators, dropped down to the Bays. The elevator was full but he was the only person in it.

"Hey Ike. Seen any ghosts yet?" Hal Bauerman said cheerfully.

"No."

"Me neither. I feel sort of left out. Here's the print on the Driver specs, with the new stuff fed in."

"Mort Laxness was seeing things up in Urban just now. He's not one I would have picked as hysterical."

"Ike," said Larane Gutierrez, the shop assistant, "nobody is hysterical. These people are here."

"What people?"

"The people from earth."

"We're all from earth, as far as I know."

"I mean the people everybody sees."

"I don't. Hal doesn't. Rod doesn't—"

"Seen some," Rod Bond muttered. "I don't know. It's real crazy, I know, Ike, but all those people that were hanging around Pueblo Corridor all day yesterday—I know you can walk through them but everybody saw them—they were like washing out a lot of cloths and wringing out the water. It was like some old tape in anthro or something."

"A group delusion—"

"—isn't what's going on," Larane snapped. She was shrill, aggressive. At any disagreement, Ike thought, she always got strident. "These people are here, Ike. And there's more of them all the time."

"So the ship is full of real people that you can walk through?"

"Good way to get a lot of people in a small space," Hal observed, with a fixed grin.

"And whatever you see is real, of course, even if I don't see it?"

"I don't know what you see," Larane said. "I don't know what's real. I know that they're here. I don't know who they are; maybe we have to find out. The ones I saw yesterday looked like they were from some really primitive culture, they had on animal skins, but they were actually kind of beautiful, the people I mean. Well fed and very alert-looking, watchful. I had a feeling for the first time they might be seeing us, not just us seeing them, but I wasn't sure."

Rod was nodding agreement.

"Next thing then is you start talking with them, then? Hi folks, welcome to Spes?"

"So far, if you get close, they just sort of aren't there, but people are getting closer," she answered quite seriously.

"Larane," Ike said, "do you hear yourself? Rod? Listen, if I came to you and said hey, guess what, a space alien with three heads has beamed aboard from his flying saucer and here he is—What's wrong? Don't you see him? Can't you see him, Larane? Rod? You don't? But I do! And you do, too, don't you, Hal, you see the three-headed space alien?"

"Sure," Hal said. "Little green bugger."

"Do you believe us?"

"No," Larane said. "Because you're lying. But we're not."

"Then you're insane."

"To deny what I and the people with me see, that would be just as insane."

"Hey, this is a really interesting ontological debate," Hal said, "but we're about twenty-five minutes overdue on the Driver specs report, folks."

Working late that night in his cube, Ike felt the soft electric thrilling along his arms and back, the sense of crowding, a murmur below the threshold of hearing, a smell of sweat or musk or human breath. He put his head in his hands for a minute, then looked up again at the Schoenfeldt screen and spoke as if talking to it. "You cannot let this happen," he said. "This is all the hope we have."

The cube was empty, the still air was odorless.

He worked on for a while. When he came to bed he lay beside his wife's deep, sleeping silence. She was as far from him as another world.

And Esther lay in the hospital in her permanent darkness. No, not permanent. Temporary. A healing darkness. She would see.

"What are you doing, Noah?"

The boy was standing at the washstand gazing down into the bowl, which was half full of water. His expression was rapt. He said, "Watching the goldfish. They came out of the tap."

"The question is this: To what extent does the concept of illusion usefully describe a shared experience with elements of interactivity?"

"Well," Jaime said, "the interactivity could itself be illusory. Joan of Arc and her voices." But there was no conviction in his own voice, and Helena, who seemed to have taken over the leadership of the Emergency Committee, pursued: "What do you think of inviting some of our guests to sit in on this meeting?"

"Hold on," Ike said. "You say 'shared experience,' but it's not a shared experience; I don't share it; there are others who don't; and what justification have you for claiming it's shared? If these phantoms, these 'guests,' are impalpable, vanish when you approach, inaudible, they're not guests, they're ghosts, you're abandoning any effort at rationality—"

"Ike, I'm sorry, but you can't deny their existence because you are unable to perceive them."

"On what sounder basis could I deny their existence?"

"But you deny that we can use the same basis for accepting it."

"Lack of hallucinations is considered the basis from which one judges another person's perceptions as hallucinations."

"Call them hallucinations, then," Helena said, "although I liked ghosts better. 'Ghosts' may be in fact quite accurate. But we don't know how to coexist with ghosts. It's not something we were trained in. We have to learn how to do it as we go along. And believe me, we have to. They are not going away. They are here, and what 'here' is is changing too. Maybe you could be very useful to us, if you were willing to be, Ike, just because you aren't aware of—of our guests, and the changes. But we who are aware of them have to learn what kind of existence they have, and why. For you to go on denying that they have any is obstructive to the work we're trying to do."

"Whom the gods would destroy they first drive mad," Ike said, getting up from his seat at the conference table. Nobody else said anything. They all looked embarrassed, looked down. He left the room in silence.

There was a group of people in CC Corridor running and laughing. "Head 'em off at the pass!" yelled a big man, Stiernen of Flight Engineering, waving his arms as if at some horde or crowd, and a woman shouted, "They're bison! They're bison! Let 'em go down C Corridor, there's more room!" Ike walked straight ahead, looking straight ahead.

"There's a vine growing by the front door," Susan said at breakfast. Her tone was so complacent that he thought nothing of it for a moment except that he was glad to hear her speak normally for once.

Then he said, "Sue—"

"What can I do about it, Ike? What do you want? You want me to lie, say nothing, pretend there isn't a vine growing there? But there is. It looks like a scarlet runner bean. It's there."

"Sue, vines grow in dirt. Earth. There is no earth in Spes."

"I know that."

"How can you both know it and deny it?"

"It's going backwards, Dad," Noah said in his new, slightly husky voice.

"What is?"

"Well, there were the people first. All those weird old women and cripples and things, remember, and then all the other kinds of people. And then there started being animals, and now plants and stuff. Wow, did you know they saw whales in the Reservoirs, Mom?"

She laughed. "I only saw the horses on the Common," she said.

"They were really pretty," Noah said.

"I didn't see them," Ike said, "I didn't see horses on the Common."

"There were a whole lot of them. They wouldn't let you get anywhere near, though. I guess they were wild. There were some really neat spotted ones. Appaloosa, Nina said."

"I didn't see horses," Ike said. He put his face in his hands and began to cry.

"Hey, Dad," he heard Noah's voice, and then Susan's, "It's OK, No. It's OK. Go on to school. It's all right, sweetie." The door hissed.

Her hands were on his head, smoothing his hair, and on his shoulders, gently rocking and shaking him. "It's OK, Ike . . . "

"No, it's not. It's not OK. It's not all right. It's all

gone crazy. It's all ruined, ruined, wasted, wrong. Gone wrong."

Susan was silent for a long time, kneading and rocking his shoulders. She said at last, "It scares me when I think about it, Ike. It seems like something supernatural, and I don't think there is anything supernatural. But if I don't think about it in words like that, if I just look at it, look at the people and the—the horses and the vine by the door—it makes sense. How did we, how could we have thought we could just leave? Who do we think we are? All it is, is we brought ourselves with us . . . The horses and the whales and the old women and the sick babies. They're just us, we're them, they're here."

He said nothing for a while. Finally he drew a long breath. "So," he said. "Go with the flow. Embrace the unexplainable. Believe because it's unbelievable. Who cares about understanding, anyhow? Who needs it? Things make a lot better sense if you just don't think about them. Maybe we could all have lobotomies and really simplify life."

She took her hands from his shoulders and moved away.

"After the lobotomy, I guess we can have electronic brain implants," she said. "And sonar headbands. So we don't bump into ghosts. Is surgery the answer to all our problems?"

He turned around then, but her back was to him.

"I'm going to the hospital," she said, and left.

"Hey! Look out!" they shouted. He did not know what they saw him walking into—a herd of sheep, a troop of naked dancing savages, a cypress swamp—he did not care. He saw the Common, the corridors, the cubes.

Noah came in to change his clothes that he said were mud-stained from tag football in the dirt that had covered all the astroturf in the Common, but Ike walked on plastic grass through dustless, germless air. He walked through the great elms and chestnuts that stood twenty meters high, not between them. He walked to the elevators and pressed the buttons and came to the Health Center.

"Oh, but Esther was released this morning!" the nurse said, smiling.

"Released?"

"Yes. The little black girl came with your wife's note, first thing this morning."

"May I see the note?"

"Sure. It's in her file, just hold on—" She handed it over. It was not a note from Susan. It was in Esther's scrawling hand, addressed to Isaac Rose. He unfolded it.

I am going up in the mountains for a while.

With love,
Esther.

Outside the Health Center he stood looking down the corridors. They ran to left, to right, and straight ahead. They were 2.2 meters high, 2.6 meters wide, painted light tan, with colored stripes on the grey floors. The blue stripes ended at the door of the Health Center, or started there, ending and starting were the same thing, but the white arrows set in the blue stripes every 3 meters pointed to the Health Center, not away from it, so they ended there, where he stood. The floors were light grey, except for the colored stripes, and perfectly smooth and almost level, for in Area 8 the curvature of Spes was barely perceptible. Lights shone from panels in the ceilings of the corridors at intervals of 5 meters. He knew all the intervals, all the specifications, all the materials, all the relationships. He had them all in his mind. He had thought about them for years. He had reasoned them. He had planned them.

Nobody could be lost in Spes. All the corridors

led to known places. You came to those places following the arrows and the colored stripes. If you followed every corridor and took every elevator, you
would never get lost and always end up safe where
you started from. And you would never stumble,
because all the floors were of smooth metal polished
and painted light grey, with colored stripes and
white arrows guiding you to the desired end.

Ike took two steps and stumbled, falling violently
forward. Under his hands was something rough,
irregular, painful. A rock, a boulder, protruded
through the smooth metal floor of the corridor. It was
dark brownish grey veined with white, pocked and
cracked; a little scurf of yellowish lichen grew near
his hands. The heel of his right hand hurt, and he
raised it to look at it. He had grazed the skin in falling
on the rock. He licked the tiny film of blood from the
graze. Squatting there, he looked at the rock and then
past it. He saw nothing but the corridor. He would
have nothing but the rock, until he found her. The
rock and the taste of his own blood. He stood up.

"Esther!"

His voice echoed faintly down the corridors.

"Esther, I can't see. Show me how to see!"

There was no answer.

He set off, walking carefully around the rock,
walking carefully forward. It was a long way and he
was never sure he was not lost. He was not sure
where he was, though the climbing got steeper and
harder and the air began to be very thin and cold.
He was not sure of anything until he heard his
mother's voice. "Isaac, dear, are you awake?" she
asked rather sharply. He turned and saw her sitting
beside Esther on an outcropping of granite beside
the steep, dusty trail. Behind them, across a great
dropping gulf of air, snow peaks shone in the high,
clear light. Esther looked at him. Her eyes were clear
also, but dark, and she said, "Now we can go down."

THE ASCENT OF THE NORTH FACE

From the diary of Simon Interthwaite of the First Love-joy Street Expedition

2/21. Robert has reached Base Camp with five Sherbets. He brought several copies of the *Times* from last month, which we devoured eagerly. Our team is now complete. Tomorrow the Advance Party goes up. Weather holds.

2/22. Accompanied Advance Party as far as the col below The Verandah before turning back. Winds up to 40 mph in gusts, but weather holds. Tonight Peter radioed all well at Verandah Camp.

The Sherbets are singing at their campfires.

2/23. Making ready. Tightened gossels. Weather holds.

2/24. Reached Verandah Camp easily in one day's climb. Tricky bit where the lattice and tongue and groove join, but Advance Party had left rope in place and we negotiated the overhang without real difficulty. Omu Ba used running jump and arrived earlier than rest of party. Inventive but undisciplined. Bad example to other Sherbets. Verandah Camp is level, dry, sheltered, far more comfortable than Base. Glad to be out of the endless rhododendrons. Snowing tonight.

2/25. Immobilized by snow.

2/26. Same.

2/27. Same. Finished last sheets of *Times* (adverts).

2/28. Derek, Nigel, Colin, and I went up in blinding snow and wind to plot course and drive pigils. Visibility very poor. Nigel whined.
  Turned back at noon, reached Verandah Camp at 3 pip emma.

2/29. Driving rain and wind. Omu Ba drunk since 2/27. What on? Stove alcohol found to be low. Inventive but undisciplined. Chastisement difficult in circumstances.

2/30. Robert roped right up to the North-East Overhang. Forced to turn back by Sherbets' dread of occupants. Insuperable superstition. We must eliminate plans for that route and go straight for the Drain Pipe. We cannot endure much longer here crowded up in this camp without newspapers. There is not room for six men in our tent, and we hear the sixteen Sherbets fighting continually in theirs. I see now that the group is unnecessarily numerous even if some are under 5 foot 2 inches in height. Ten men, handpicked, would be enough. Visibility zero all day. Snow, rain, wind.

2/31. Hail, sleet, fog. Three Sherbets have gone missing.

3/1. Out of Bovril. Derek very low.

3/4. Missed entries during blizzard. Today bright sun, no wind. Snow dazzling on lower elevations; from here we cannot see the heights. Sherbets returned from unexplained absence with Ovaltine. Spirits high. Digging out and making ready all day for ascent (two groups) tomorrow.

3/5. Success! We are on the Verandah Roof! View overwhelming. Unattained summit of 2618 clearly visible in the SE. Second Party (Peter, Robert, eight Sherbets) not here yet. Windy and exposed campsite on steep slope. Shingles slippery with rain and sleet.

3/6. Nigel and two Sherbets went back down to the North Edge to meet Second Party. Returned 4 pip emma without having sighted them. They must have been delayed at Verandah Camp. Anxiety. Radio silent. Wind rising.

3/7. Colin strained shoulder on rope climbing up to the Window. Stupid, childish prank. Whether or not there are occupants, the Sherbets are very strong on not disturbing them. No sign of Second Party. Radio messages enigmatic, constant interference from KWJJ Country Music Station. Windy, but clear weather holds.

3/8. Resolved to go up tomorrow if weather holds. Mended doggles, replaced worn pigil-holders. Sherbets noncommittal.

3/9. I am alone on the High Roof.
  No one else willing to continue ascent. Colin and Nigel will wait for me three days at Verandah Roof Camp; Derek and four Sherbets began descent to Base. I set off with two Sherbets at 5 ack emma. Fine sunrise, in East, at 7.04 ack emma. Climbed steadily all day. Tricky bit at last overhang. Sherbets very plucky. Omu Ba while swinging on rope said,

"Observe fine view, sah!" Exhausted at arrival at
High Roof Camp, but the three advance Sherbets had
tents set up and Ovaltine ready. Slope so steep here I
feel I may roll off in my sleep!

Sherbets singing in their tent.

Above me the sharp Summit, and the Chimney
rising sheer against the stars.

*That is the last entry in Simon Interthwaite's journal.
Four of the five Sherbets with him at the High Roof
Camp returned after three days to the Base Camp. They
brought the journal, two clean vests, and a tube of
anchovy paste back with them. Their report of his fate
was incoherent. The Interthwaite Party abandoned the
attempt to scale the North Face of 2647 Lovejoy Street
and returned to Calcutta.*

*In 1980 a Japanese party of Izutsu employees with
four Sherbet guides attained the summit by a North
Face route, rappelling across the study windows and
driving pitons clear up to the eaves. Occupant protest
was ineffective.*

No one has yet climbed the Chimney.

THE ROCK THAT CHANGED THINGS

A nurobl called Bu, working one day with her crew on the rockpile of Obling College, found the rock that changed things.

Where the obls live, the shores of the river are rocky. Boulders, large stones, small stones, pebbles, and gravel lie piled and scattered for miles up and down the banks. The towns of the obls are built of stone; they hunt the rock-coney for their meat feasts. Their nurobls gather and prepare stonecrop and lichen for ordinary food, and build the houses and the colleges, and keep them neat, for the obls grow nervous and unhappy when things are not kept in order.

The heart of an obl town is its college, and the pride of every college is its terraces, which shelve down towards the river from the high stone buildings. The stones of the terraces are arranged according to size: boulders make the outer walls, and within them are rows of large rocks, then banks of small stones, and at last the inner terraces of pebbles set in elaborate mosaics and patterns in gravel. On the terraces the obls stroll and sit in the long, warm days, smoking ta-leaf in pipes of soapstone, and discussing history, natural history, philosophy, and metaphysics. So long as the rocks are arranged in order of shape and size and the patterns are kept clear and tidy, the obls have peace of mind and can think deeply. After their conversations on the terraces, the wisest old obls enter the colleges and write down the best of what was thought and said, in the Books of Record that are kept neatly ranged on the shelves of the college libraries.

When the river floods in early spring and rises up the terraces, tumbling the rocks about, washing the gravel away, and causing great disorder, the obls stay inside the colleges. There they read the Books of Record, discuss and annotate, plan new designs for the terraces, eat meat feasts, and smoke. Their nurs cook and serve the feasts and keep the rooms of the colleges orderly. As soon as the floods pass, the nurs begin to sort the rocks and straighten up the terraces. They hurry to do so because the disorder left by the floods makes the obls very nervous, and when they are nervous they beat and rape the nurs more harshly than usual.

The spring floods this year had broken through the boulder wall of the town of Obling, leaving branches and driftwood and other litter on the terraces and disturbing or destroying many of the patterns. The terraces of Obling College are notable for the perfect order and complex beauty of their pebble-patterns. Famous obls have spent years of their lives designing the patterns and choosing the stones; one great designer, Aknegni, is said to have worked with his own hands to perfect his creation. If a single pebble is lost from such a design, the nurobls will spend days hunting through the rockpiles for a replacement of precisely the right shape and size. On such a task the nurobl called Bu was engaged, along with her crew, when she came upon the stone that changed things.

When replacement rocks are needed, the rock-pile nurs often make a rough copy of that section of the terrace mosaic, so that they can test pebbles in it for fit without carrying them all the way up to the inner terraces. Bu had placed a trial stone in a test pattern in this fashion, and was gazing at it to be sure the size and shape were exact, when she was struck by a quality of the stone which she had never noticed before: the color. The pebbles of this part of the design were all large ovals, a palm-and-a-quarter wide and a palm-and-a-half long. The rock Bu had just set into the test pattern was a perfect "quarter-half" oval, and so fit exactly; but while the other rocks were mostly a dark, smooth-grained bluish grey, the new one was a vivid blue-green, with flecks of paler jade green.

Bu knew, of course, that the color of a rock is a matter of absolute indifference, an accidental and trivial quality that does not affect the true pattern in any way. All the same, she found herself gazing with peculiar satisfaction at this blue-green stone. Presently she thought, "This stone is beautiful." She was not looking, as she should have been, at the whole design, but at the one stone, whose color was set off by the duller hue of the others. She was strangely moved; strange thoughts arose in her mind. She thought, "This stone is significant. It means. It is a word." She picked it up and held it while studying the test pattern.

The original design, up on the terrace, was called the Dean's Design, for the Dean of the College, Festl, who had planned this section of the terraces. When Bu replaced the blue-green stone in the pattern, it still caught her eye by its color, distracting her mind from the pattern, but she could not see any meaning in it.

She took the blue-green stone to the rockpile fore-nur and asked him if he saw anything wrong, or odd, or particular about the stone. The fore-nur gazed thoughtfully at the stone, but at last opened his eyes wide, meaning no.

Bu took the stone up to the inner terraces and set it into the true pattern. It fitted the Dean's Design exactly; its shape and size were perfect. But, standing back to study the pattern, Bu thought it scarcely seemed to be the Dean's Design at all. It was not that the new stone changed the design; it simply completed a pattern that Bu had never realized was there: a pattern of color, that had little or no relation to the shape-and-size arrangement of the Dean's Design. The new stone completed a spiral of blue-green stones within the field of interlocked rhomboids of "quarter-half" ovals that formed the center of Festl's design. Most of the blue-green stones were ones that Bu had laid over the past several years; but the spiral had been begun by some other nur, before Bu was promoted to the Dean's Design.

Just then Dean Festl came strolling out in the spring sunshine, his rusty gun on his shoulder, his pipe in his mouth, happy to see the disorder of the floods being repaired. The Dean was a kind old obl who had never raped Bu, though he often patted her. Bu summoned up her courage, hid her eyes, and said, "Lord Dean, sir! Would the Lord Dean in his knowledge be so good as to tell me the verbal significance of this section of the true pattern which I have just repaired?"

Dean Festl paused, perhaps a touch displeased to be interrupted in his meditations; but seeing the young nur so modestly crouching and hiding all her eyes, he patted her in a forebearing way and said, "Certainly. This subsection of my design may be read, on the simplest level, as: 'I place stones beautifully,' or 'I place stones in excellent order.' There is an immanent higher-plane postverbal significance, of course, as well as the Ineffable Arcana. But you needn't bother your little head with that!"

"Is it possible," the nur asked in a submissive voice, "to find a meaning in the *colors* of the stones?"

The Dean smiled again and patted her in several places. "Who knows what goes on in the heads of nurs! Color! Meaning in color! Now run along, little nurblit. You've done very pretty repair work here. Very neat, very nice." And he strolled on, puffing on his pipe and enjoying the spring sunshine.

Bu returned to the rockpile to sort stones, but her mind was disturbed. All night she dreamed of the blue-green rock. In the dream the rock spoke, and the rocks about it in the pattern began speaking too. Waking, Bu could not remember the words the stones had said.

The sun was not up yet, but the nurs were; and Bu spoke to several of her nestmates and work-friends while they fed and cleaned the blits and ate their hurried breakfast of cold fried lichen. "Come up onto the terraces, now, before the obls are up," Bu said. "I want to show you something."

Bu had many friends, and eight or nine nurs followed her up onto the terraces, some of them bringing their nursing or toddling blits along. "What's Bu got in her head this time!" they said to each other, laughing.

"Now look," Bu said when they were all on the part of the inner terrace that Dean Festl had designed. "Look at the patterns. And look at the *colors* of the rocks."

"Colors don't mean anything," said one nur, and another, "Colors aren't part of the patterns, Bu."

"But what if they were?" said Bu. "Just look."

The nurs, being used to silence and obedience, looked.

"Well," said one of them after a while. "Isn't that amazing!"

"Look at that!" said Bu's best friend, Ko. "That spiral of blue-green running all over the Dean's

Design! And there's five red hematites around a yellow sandstone—like a flower."

"This whole section in brown basalt—it cuts across the—the real pattern, doesn't it?" said little Ga.

"It makes another pattern. A different pattern," Bu said. "Maybe it makes an immanent pattern of ineffable significance."

"Oh, come off it, Bu," said Ko. "You a Professor or something?"

The others laughed, but Bu was too excited to see that she was funny. "No," she said earnestly, "but look—that blue-green rock, there, the last one in the spiral."

"Serpentinite," said Ko.

"Yes, I know. But if the Dean's Design means something—He said that that part means 'I place stones beautifully'—Well, could the blue-green rock be a different word? With a different meaning?"

"What meaning?"

"I don't know. I thought you might know." Bu looked hopefully at Un, an elderly nur who, though he had been lamed in a rockslide in his youth, was so good at fine pattern-maintenance that the obls had let him live. Un stared at the blue-green stone, and at the curve of blue-green stones, and at last said slowly, "It might say, 'The nur places stones.'"

"What nur?" Ko asked.

"Bu," little Ga said. "She did place the stone."

Bu and Un both opened their eyes wide, to signify No.

"Patterns aren't ever about nurs!" said Ko.

"Maybe patterns made of colors are," said Bu, getting excited and blinking very fast.

"The nur," said Ko, following the blue-green curve with all three eyes, "—'the nur places stones beautifully in uncontrollable loopingness.' My goodness! What's that all about?" He read on along the curve—" 'in uncontrollable loopingness fore,' what's that? Oh, 'foreshadowing the seen.' "

"'The vision,'" Un suggested. "'The vision of . . .'
I don't know the last word."

"Are you seeing all that in the colors of the
rocks?" asked Ga, amazed.

"In the patterns of the colors," Bu replied. "They
aren't accidental. Not meaningless. All the time, we
have been putting them here in patterns—not just
ones the obls design and we execute, but other patterns—nur patterns—with new meanings. Look—look
at them!"

Since they were used to silence and obedience,
they all stood and looked at the patterns on the
inner terraces of the College of Obling. They saw
how the arrangement by shape and size of the pebbles and larger stones made regular squares,
oblongs, triangles, dodecahedrons, zigzags, and rec-
tilinear designs of great and orderly beauty and significance. And they saw how the arrangement of the
stones by color had created other designs, less complete, often merely sketched or hinted—circles, spirals, ovals, and complex curvilinear mazes and
labyrinths of great and unpredictable beauty and
significance. So a long loop of white quartzites cut
right across the quarter-palm straight-edge double
line; and the rhomboid section of half-palm sand-
stones seemed to be an element in a long crescent of
pale yellow.

Both patterns were there; did one cancel the
other, or was each part of the other? It was difficult
to see them both at once, but not impossible.

After a long time little Ga asked, "Did we do all
that without even knowing we were doing it?"

"I always looked at the colors of the rocks," Un
said in a low voice, looking down.

"So did I," Ko said. "And the grain and texture,
too. I started that wiggly part in the Crystal Angles,"
pointing at a very ancient and famous section of the
terrace, designed by the great OholothL. "Last year,

after the late flood, when we lost so many stones from the design, remember? I got a lot of amethysts from the Ubi Caves. I love purple!" His tone was defiant.

Bu looked at a circle of small, smooth turquoises inlaid in a corner of a set of interlocked rectangles. "I like blue-green," Bu said in a whisper. "I like blue-green. He likes purple. We see the colors of the stones. We make the pattern. We make the pattern beautifully."

"Should we tell the Professors, do you think?" little Ga asked, getting excited. "They might give us extra food."

Old Un opened all his eyes very wide. "Don't breathe a word of this to the Professors! They don't like patterns to change. You know that. It makes them nervous. They might get nervous and punish us."

"We are not afraid," Bu said, in a whisper.

"They wouldn't understand," Ko said. "They don't look at colors. They don't listen to us. And if they did, they'd know it was just nurs talking and didn't mean anything. Wouldn't they? But I'm going back to the Caves and get some more amethysts and finish that wiggly part," pointing to the Crystal Angles, where repairs had scarcely begun. "They'll never even see it."

Ga's naughty little blit, Professor Endl's son, was digging up pebbles from the Superior Triangle, and had to be spanked. "Oh," Ga sighed, "he's all oblblit! I just don't know what to do with him."

"He'll go to School next year," Un said drily. "They'll know what to do with him."

"But what will I do without him?" said Ga.

The sun was well up in the sky now, and Professors could be seen looking out from their bedroom windows over the terraces. They would not like to see nurs loitering, and small blits were, of course, absolutely forbidden within the college walls. Bu and the others hastily returned to the nests and workhouses.

*   *   *

Ko went to the Ubi Caves that same day, and Bu
went along; they came back with sacks of fine
amethysts, and worked for several days completing
the wiggly part, which they called the Purple
Waves, in the repair and maintenance of the Crystal
Angles. Ko was happy in the work, and sang and
joked, and at night he and Bu made love. But Bu
remained preoccupied. She kept studying the patterns of color on the terraces, and finding more and
more of them, and more and more meanings and
ideas in them.

"Are they all about nurs?" old Un asked. His
arthritis kept him from the terraces, but Bu reported
her findings to him every day.

"No," Bu said, "most of them are about obls and
nurs both. And blits, too. But nurs made them. So
they're different. Obl patterns are never really about
nurs. Only about obls and what obls think. But
when you begin to read the colors they say the most
interesting things!"

Bu was so excited and persuasive that other
nurs of Obling began studying the color patterns,
learning how to read their meanings. The practice
spread to other nests, and soon to other towns.
Before long, nurs all up and down the river were dis-
covering that their terraces, too, were full of wild
designs in colored stones, and surprising messages
concerning obls, nurs, and blits.

Many nurs, however, upset by the whole idea,
steadfastly refused to see patterns in color or to
allow that the color of a stone could have any significance at all. "The obls count on us not to change
things," these nurs said. "We are their nurobls.
They depend on us to keep their patterns neat, and
keep the blits quiet, and maintain order, so that
they can do important work. If we start inventing

new meanings, changing things, disturbing the patterns, where will it end? It isn't fair to the obls."

Bu, however, would hear none of that; she was full of her discovery. She no longer listened in silence. She spoke. She went about among the workhouses, speaking. And one evening, summoning up her courage, and wearing around her neck on a thong a perfect, polished turquoise that she called her selfstone, she went up onto the terraces. She crossed the terraces among the startled Professors, and came to the Rectory Mosaic, where Astl the Rectoress, a famous scholar, strolled in solitary meditation, her ancient rifle slung on her back, wreaths of smoke trailing from her reeking pipe. Not even a Full Professor would have interrupted the Rectoress at such a sacred time. But Bu went straight to her, crouched, covered her eyes, and said in a tremulous but clear voice, "Lady Rectoress, ma'am! Would the Lady Rectoress in her kindness answer a question I have?"

The Rectoress was truly displeased and upset by this disorderly behavior. She turned to the nearest Professor and said, "This nur is insane; have it removed, please."

Bu was sentenced to ten days in jail, to be raped by Students whenever they pleased, and then sent to the flagstone quarries for a hundred days.

When she returned to the nest, she was pregnant from one of the rapes, and quite thin from working in the quarries, but she still wore her turquoise stone. All her nest-mates and work-friends greeted her, singing songs which they had made out of the meanings of the colored patterns on the terraces. Ko comforted her with tender affection that night, and told her that her blit would be his blit, and her nest his nest.

Not many days after, she entered the college (via the kitchens), and made her way (with the assistance of the serving-nurs) to the private room of the Canon.

The Canon of Obling College was a very old obl, renowned for his knowledge of metaphysical linguistics. He woke slowly, mornings. This morning he woke slowly and gazed with some puzzlement at the serving-nur which had come to open his curtains and serve his breakfast. It seemed to be a different one. He almost reached for his gun, but was too sleepy.

"Hullo," he said. "You're new, aren't you?"

"I want you to answer a question I have," said the nur.

The Canon woke further, and stared at this amazing creature. "At least have the decency to cover your eyes, nur!" he said, but he was not really very upset. He was so old that he was no longer quite sure what the patterns were, and so a change in them did not trouble him as much as it might have done.

"Nobody else can answer me," said the nur. "Please do. Do you know if a blue-green stone in a pattern might be a word?"

"Oh, yes, indeed," said the Canon, becoming alert. "Although, of course, all verbal color-significance is long obsolete. Of mere antiquarian interest, to old fuddy-duddies such as myself, ha. Hue-words don't occur even in the most archaic patterns. Only in the most ancient Books of Record."

"What does it mean?"

The Canon wondered if he were dreaming—discussing historical linguistics with a nur, before breakfast!—But it was an entertaining dream. "The hue of blue-green—such as that stone you seem to be wearing as an ornament—might, in its adjectival form within a pattern, have indicated a quality of untrammeled volition. As a noun, the color would have functioned to signify, how shall I put it?—an absence of coercion; a lack of control; a condition of self-determination—"

"Freedom," the nur said. "Does it mean freedom?"

"No, my dear," said the Canon. "It did. But it does not."

"Why?"

"Because the word is obsolete," said the Canon, beginning to tire of this inexplicable dialogue. "Now go away like a good nur and tell my servant to bring my breakfast."

"Look out the window," the wild-eyed nur said, in so passionate a voice that the Canon was quite alarmed. "Look out the window at the terraces! Look at the colors of the stones! Look at the patterns the nurs make, the designs we have made, the meanings we have written! Look for the freedom! Oh please do look!"

And with that final plea, the amazing apparition vanished. The Canon lay staring at his bedroom door; and in a moment it opened. His old serving-nur came in with his tray of stonecrop tea and smoking hot kippered lichen. "Good morning, Lord Canon, sir!" she said cheerfully. "Awake already? A lovely morning!" And after setting down the tray by his bed, she swept the curtains open wide.

"Was there a young nur in here just now?" the Canon asked, rather nervously.

"Certainly not, sir. At least, not that I know of," said the serving-nur. But did she for a moment glance quite directly, knowingly—did she have the audacity to *look* at him—? Surely not. "Lovely the terraces are this morning," she went on. "Your Canonitude ought to have a look."

"Get out, out," the Canon growled, and the nur left with a demure curtsy, covering her eyes.

The Canon ate his breakfast in bed and then got up. He went to the window to look out on the terraces of his college in the morning light.

For a moment he thought he was dreaming again, seeing entirely different patterns than those he had seen all his long life on those terraces—wild designs of curves and colors, amazing phrases, unimagined significances, a wonderful newness of meaning and beauty—and then he opened all his eyes wide, very wide, and blinked; and it was gone. The familiar, true order of the terraces lay clear and regular in the morning light. And there was nothing else to see. The Canon turned away from the window and opened a book.

So he did not see the long line of nurobls coming up from the nests and workhouses down below the boulder walls, carrying blits and dancing as they came, dancing and singing across the terraces. He heard the singing, but only as a noise without significance. It was not until the first rock flew through his window that he looked up and cried out in agitation, "What is the meaning of this?"

THE KERASTION

For Roussel Sargent, who invented it

The small caste of the Tanners was a sacred one. To
eat food prepared by a Tanner would entail a year's
purification to a Tinker or a Sculptor, and even low-
power castes such as the Traders had to be cleansed
by a night's ablutions after dealing for leather goods.
Chumo had been a Tanner since she was five years
old and had heard the willows whisper all night long
at the Singing Sands. She had had her proving day,
and since then had worn a Tanner's madder-red and
blue shirt and doublet, woven of linen on a willow-
wood loom. She had made her masterpiece, and since
then had worn the Master Tanner's neckband of
dried vauti-tuber incised with the double line and
double circles. So clothed and so ornamented she
stood among the willows by the burying ground,
waiting for the funeral procession of her brother,
who had broken the law and betrayed his caste. She
stood erect and silent, gazing towards the village by
the river and listening for the drum.

She did not think; she did not want to think. But
she saw her brother Kwatewa in the reeds down by

the river, running ahead of her, a little boy too young to have caste, too young to be polluted by the sacred, a crazy little boy pouncing on her out of the tall reeds shouting, "I'm a mountain lion!"

A serious little boy watching the river run, asking, "Does it ever stop? Why can't it stop running, Chumo?"

A five-year-old coming back from the Singing Sands, coming straight to her, bringing her the joy, the crazy, serious joy that shone in his round face— "Chumo! I heard the sand singing! I heard it! I have to be a Sculptor, Chumo!"

She had stood still. She had not held out her arms. And he had checked his run towards her and stood still, the light going out of his face. She was only his wombsister. He would have truesibs, now. He and she were of different castes. They would not touch again.

Ten years after that day she had come with most of the townsfolk to Kwatewa's proving day, to see the sand-sculpture he had made in the Great Plain Place where the Sculptors performed their art. Not a breath of wind had yet rounded off the keen edges or leveled the lovely curves of the classic form he had executed with such verve and sureness, the Body of Amakumo. She saw admiration and envy in the faces of his true-brothers and truesisters. Standing aside among the sacred castes, she heard the speaker of the Sculptors dedicate Kwatewa's proving piece to Amakumo. As his voice ceased a wind came out of the desert north, Amakumo's wind, the maker hungry for the made— Amakumo the Mother eating her body, eating herself. Even while they watched, the wind destroyed Kwatewa's sculpture. Soon there was only a shapeless lump and a feathering of white sand blown across the proving ground. Beauty had gone back to the Mother. That the sculpture had been destroyed so soon and so utterly was a great honor to the maker.

The funeral procession was approaching. She

heard or imagined she heard the drumbeat, soft, no
more than a heartbeat.

Her own proving piece had been the traditional
one for Tanner women, a drumhead. Not a funeral
drum but a dancing drum, loud, gaudy with red paint
and tassels. "Your drumhead, your maidenhead!" her
truebrothers called it, and made fierce teasing jokes,
but they couldn't make her blush. Tanners had no
business blushing. They were outside shame. It had
been an excellent drum, chosen at once from the proving ground by an old Musician, who had played it so
much she soon wore off the bright paint and lost the
red tassels; but the drumhead lasted through the winter and till the Roppi Ceremony, when it finally split
wide open during the drumming for the all-night
dancing under the moons, when Chumo and Karwa
first twined their wristplaits. Chumo had been proud
all winter when she heard the voice of her drum loud
and clear across the dancing ground, she had been
proud when it split and gave itself to the Mother; but
that had been nothing to the pride she had felt in Kwatewa's sculptures. For if the work be well done and the
thing made be powerful, it belongs to the Mother. She
will desire it; she will not wait for it to give itself, but
will take it. So the child dying young is called the
Mother's Child. Beauty, the most sacred of all things,
is hers; the body of the Mother is the most beautiful of
all things. So all that is made in the likeness of the
Mother is made in sand.

To keep your work, to try to keep it for yourself,
to take her body from her, Kwatewa! How could you,
how could you, my brother? her heart said. But she
put the question back into the silence and stood
silent among the willows, the trees sacred to her
caste, watching the funeral procession come
between the flaxfields. It was his shame, not hers.
What was shame to a Tanner? It was pride she felt,
pride. For that was her masterpiece that Dastuye the

Musician held now and raised to his lips as he walked before the procession, guiding the new ghost to its body's grave.

She had made that instrument, the kerastion, the flute that is played only at a funeral. The kerastion is made of leather, and the leather is tanned human skin, and the skin is that of the wombmother or the foremother of the dead.

When Wekuri, wombmother of Chumo and Kwatewa, had died two winters ago, Chumo the Tanner had claimed her privilege. There had been an old, old kerastion to play at Wekuri's funeral, handed down from her grandmothers; but the Musician, when he had finished playing it, laid it on the mats that wrapped Wekuri in the open grave. For the night before, Chumo had flayed the left arm of the body, singing the songs of power of her caste as she worked, the songs that ask the dead mother to put her voice, her song into the instrument. She had kept and cured the piece of rawhide, rubbing it with the secret cures, wrapping it round a clay cylinder to harden, wetting it, oiling it, forming it and refining its form, till the clay went to powder and was knocked from the tube, which she then cleaned and rubbed and oiled and finished. It was a privilege which only the most powerful, the most truly shameless of the Tanners took, to make a kerastion of the mother's skin. Chumo had claimed it without fear or doubt. As she worked she had many times pictured the Musician leading the procession, playing the flute, guiding her own spirit to its grave. She had wondered which of the Musicians it might be, and who would follow her, walking in her funeral procession. Never once had she thought that it would be played for Kwatewa before it was played for her. How was she to think of him, so much younger, dying first?

He had killed himself out of shame. He had cut

his wrist veins with one of the tools he had made to cut stone.

His death itself was no shame, since there had been nothing for him to do but die. There was no fine, no ablution, no purification, for what he had done.

Shepherds had found the cave where he had kept the stones, great marble pieces from the cave walls, carved into copies of his own sandsculptures, his own sacred work for the Solstice and the Hariba: sculptures of stone, abominable, durable, desecrations of the body of the Mother.

People of his caste had destroyed the things with hammers, beaten them to dust and sand, swept the sand down into the river. She had thought Kwatewa would follow them, but he had gone to the cave at night and taken the sharp tool and cut his wrists and let his blood run. Why can't it stop running, Chumo?

The Musician had come abreast of her now as she stood among the willows by the burying ground. Dastuye was old and skillful; his slow dancewalk seemed to float him above the ground in rhythm with the soft heartbeat of the drum that followed. Guiding the spirit and the body on its litter borne by four casteless men, he played the kerastion. His lips lay light on the leather mouthpiece, his fingers moved lightly as he played, and there was no sound at all. The kerastion flute has no stops and both its ends are plugged with disks of bronze. Tunes played on it are not heard by living ears. Chumo, listening, heard the drum and the whisper of the north wind in the willow leaves. Only Kwatewa in his woven grass shroud on the litter heard what song the Musician played for him, and knew whether it was a song of shame, or of grief, or of welcome.

THE SHOBIES' STORY

They met at Ve Port more than a month before their
first flight together, and there, calling themselves
after their ship as most crews did, became the
Shobies. Their first consensual decision was to
spend their isyeye in the coastal village of Liden, on
Hain, where the negative ions could do their thing.

Liden was a fishing port with an eighty-thousand-
year history and a population of four hundred. Its
fisherfolk farmed the rich shoal waters of their bay,
shipped the catch inland to the cities, and managed
the Liden Resort for vacationers and tourists and
new space crews on isyeye (the word is Hainish and
means "making a beginning together," or "beginning to be together," or, used technically, "the period of time and area of space in which a group forms
if it is going to form." A honeymoon is an isyeye of
two). The fisherwomen and fishermen of Liden
were as weathered as driftwood and about as
talkative. Six-year-old Asten, who had misunder-
stood slightly, asked one of them if they were all
eighty thousand years old. "Nope," she said.

Like most crews, the Shobies used Hainish as
their common language. So the name of the one

Hainish crew member, Sweet Today, carried its meaning as words as well as name, and at first seemed a silly thing to call a big, tall, heavy woman in her late fifties, imposing of carriage and almost as taciturn as the villagers. But her reserve proved to be a deep well of congeniality and tact, to be called upon as needed, and her name soon began to sound quite right. She had family—all Hainish have family— kinfolk of all denominations, grandchildren and cross-cousins, affines and cosines, scattered all over the Ekumen, but no relatives in this crew. She asked to be Grandmother to Rig, Asten, and Betton, and was accepted.

The only Shoby older than Sweet Today was the Terran Lidi, who was seventy-two EYs and not interested in grandmothering. Lidi had been navigating for fifty years, and there was nothing she didn't know about NAFAL ships, although occasionally she forgot that their ship was the *Shoby* and called it the *Soso* or the *Alterra*. And there were things she didn't know, none of them knew, about the *Shoby*.

They talked, as human beings do, about what they didn't know.

Churten theory was the main topic of conversation, evenings at the driftwood fire on the beach after dinner. The adults had read whatever there was to read about it, of course, before they ever volunteered for the test mission. Gveter had more recent information and presumably a better understanding of it than the others, but it had to be pried out of him. Only twenty-five, the only Cetian in the crew, much hairier than the others, and not gifted in language, he spent a lot of time on the defensive. Assuming that as an Anarresti he was more proficient at mutual aid and more adept at cooperation than the others, he lectured them about their propertarian habits; but he held tight to his knowledge, because he needed the advantage it gave him. For a while he would speak only in negatives: don't call it the churten "drive," it isn't a drive, don't call it the churten "effect," it isn't an effect. What is it, then? A long lecture ensued, beginning with the rebirth of Cetian physics since the revision of Shevekian temporalism by the Intervalists, and ending with the general conceptual framework of the churten. Everyone listened very carefully, and finally Sweet Today spoke, carefully. "So the ship will be moved," she said, "by ideas?"

"No, no, no, no," said Gveter. But he hesitated for the next word so long that Karth asked a question: "Well, you haven't actually talked about any physical, material events or effects at all." The question was characteristically indirect. Karth and Oreth, the Gethenians who with their two children were the affective focus of the crew, the "hearth" of it, in their terms, came from a not very theoretically minded subculture, and knew it. Gveter could run rings round them with his Cetian physico-philosophico-techno-natter. He did so at once. His accent did not make his explanations any clearer. He went on about coherence and meta-intervals, and at last demanded, with gestures of despair, "Khow can I say it in Khainish? No! It is not physical, it is not not physical, these are the categories our minds must discard entirely, this is the khole point!"

"Buth-buth-buth-buth-buth-buth," went Asten, softly, passing behind the half circle of adults at the driftwood fire on the wide, twilit beach. Rig followed, also going, "Buth-buth-buth-buth," but louder. They were being spaceships, to judge from their maneuvers around a dune and their communications— "Locked in orbit, Navigator!"—But the noise they were imitating was the noise of the little fishing boats of Liden putt-putting out to sea.

"I crashed!" Rig shouted, flailing in the sand. "Help! Help! I crashed!"

"Hold on, Ship Two!" Asten cried. "I'll rescue you! Don't breathe! Oh, oh, trouble with the Churten Drive! Buth-buth-ack! Ack! Brrrrmmm-ack-ack-ack-rrrrrmmmmm, buth-buth-buth-buth. . . ."

They were six and four EYs old. Tai's son Betton, who was eleven, sat at the driftwood fire with the adults, though at the moment he was watching Rig and Asten as if he wouldn't mind taking off to help rescue Ship Two. The little Gethenians had spent more time on ships than on planet, and Asten liked to boast about being "actually fifty-eight," but this was Betton's first crew, and his only NAFAL flight had been from Terra to Hain. He and his biomother, Tai, had lived in a reclamation commune on Terra. When she had drawn the lot for Ekumenical service, and requested training for ship duty, he had asked her to bring him as family. She had agreed; but after training, when she volunteered for this test flight, she had tried to get Betton to withdraw, to stay in training or go home. He had refused. Shan, who had trained with them, told the others this, because the tension between the mother and son had to be understood to be used effectively in group formation. Betton had requested to come, and Tai had given in, but plainly not with an undivided will. Her relationship to the boy was cool and mannered. Shan offered him fatherly-brotherly warmth, but Betton accepted it sparingly, coolly, and sought no formal crew relation with him or anyone.

Ship Two was being rescued, and attention returned to the discussion. "All right," said Lidi. "We know that anything that goes faster than light, any *thing* that goes faster than light, by so doing transcends the material/immaterial category—that's how we got the ansible, by distinguishing the message from the medium. But if we, the crew, are going to travel as messages, I want to understand *how*."

Gveter tore his hair. There was plenty to tear. It

grew fine and thick, a mane on his head, a pelt on his limbs and body, a silvery nimbus on his hands and face. The fuzz on his feet was, at the moment, full of sand. "Khow!" he cried. "I'm trying to tell you khow! Message, information, no no no, that's old, that's ansible technology. This is transilience! Because the field is to be conceived as the virtual field, in which the unreal interval becomes virtually effective through the mediary coherence—don't you see?"

"No," Lidi said. "What do you mean by mediary?"

After several more bonfires on the beach, the consensus opinion was that churten theory was accessible only to minds very highly trained in Cetian temporal physics. There was a less freely voiced conviction that the engineers who had built the *Shoby*'s churten apparatus did not entirely understand how it worked. Or, more precisely, what it did when it worked. That it worked was certain. The *Shoby* was the fourth ship it had been tested with, using robot crew; so far sixty-two instantaneous trips, or transiliences, had been effected between points from four hundred kilometers to twenty-seven light-years apart, with stopovers of varying lengths. Gveter and Lidi steadfastly maintained that this proved that the engineers knew perfectly well what they were doing, and that for the rest of them the seeming difficulty of the theory was only the difficulty human minds had in grasping a genuinely new concept.

"Like the circulation of the blood," said Tai. "People went around with their hearts beating for a long time before they understood why." She did not look satisfied with her own analogy, and when Shan said, "The heart has its reasons, which reason does not know," she looked offended. "Mysticism," she said, in the tone of voice of one warning a companion about dog-shit on the path.

"Surely there's nothing *beyond* understanding in

this process," Oreth said, somewhat tentatively. "Nothing that can't be understood, and reproduced."

"And quantified," Gveter said stoutly.

"But, even if people understand the process, nobody knows the human response to it—the *experience* of it. Right? So we are to report on that."

"Why shouldn't it be just like NAFAL flight, only even faster?" Betton asked.

"Because it is totally different," said Gveter.

"What could happen to us?"

Some of the adults had discussed possibilities, all of them had considered them; Karth and Oreth had talked it over in appropriate terms with their children; but evidently Betton had not been included in such discussions.

"We don't know," Tai said sharply. "I told you that at the start, Betton."

"Most likely it will be like NAFAL flight," said Shan, "but the first people who flew NAFAL didn't know what it would be like, and had to find out the physical and psychic effects—"

"The worst thing," said Sweet Today in her slow, comfortable voice, "would be that we would die. Other living beings have been on some of the test flights. Crickets. And intelligent ritual animals on the last two *Shoby* tests. They were all right." It was a very long statement for Sweet Today, and carried proportional weight.

"We are almost certain," said Gveter, "that no temporal rearrangement is involved in churten, as it is in NAFAL. And mass is involved only in terms of needing a certain core mass, just as for ansible transmission, but not in itself. So maybe even a pregnant person could be a transilient."

"They can't go on ships," Asten said. "The unborn dies if they do."

Asten was half lying across Oreth's lap; Rig, thumb in mouth, was asleep on Karth's lap.

"When we were Oneblins," Asten went on, sitting up, "there were ritual animals with our crew. Some fish and some Terran cats and a whole lot of Hainish gholes. We got to play with them. And we helped thank the ghole that they tested for lithovirus. But it didn't die. It bit Shapi. The cats slept with us. But one of them went into kemmer and got pregnant, and then the *Oneblin* had to go to Hain, and she had to have an abortion, or all her unborns would have died inside her and killed her too. Nobody knew a ritual for her, to explain to her. But I fed her some extra food. And Rig cried."

"Other people I know cried too," Karth said, stroking the child's hair.

"You tell good stories, Asten," Sweet Today observed.

"So we're sort of ritual humans," said Betton.

"Volunteers," Tai said.

"Experimenters," said Lidi.

"Experiencers," said Shan.

"Explorers," Oreth said.

"Gamblers," said Karth.

The boy looked from one face to the next.

"You know," Shan said, "back in the time of the League, early in NAFAL flight, they were sending out ships to really distant systems—trying to explore everything—crews that wouldn't come back for centuries. Maybe some of them are still out there. But some of them came back after four, five, six hundred years, and they were all mad. Crazy!" He paused dramatically. "But they were all crazy when they started. Unstable people. They had to be crazy to volunteer for a time dilation like that. What a way to pick a crew, eh?" He laughed.

"Are we stable?" said Oreth. "I like instability. I like this job. I like the risk, taking the risk together. High stakes! That's the edge of it, the sweetness of it."

Karth looked down at their children, and smiled.

"Yes. Together," Gveter said. "You aren't crazy. You are good. I love you. We are ammari."

"Ammar," the others said to him, confirming this unexpected declaration. The young man scowled with pleasure, jumped up, and pulled off his shirt. "I want to swim. Come on, Betton. Come on swimming!" he said, and ran off towards the dark, vast waters that moved softly beyond the ruddy haze of their fire. The boy hesitated, then shed his shirt and sandals and followed. Shan pulled up Tai, and they followed; and finally the two old women went off into the night and the breakers, rolling up their pants legs, laughing at themselves.

To Gethenians, even on a warm summer night on a warm summer world, the sea is no friend. The fire is where you stay. Oreth and Asten moved closer to Karth and watched the flames, listening to the faint voices out in the glimmering surf, now and then talking quietly in their own tongue, while the little sisterbrother slept on.

After thirty lazy days at Liden the Shobies caught the fish train inland to the city, where a Fleet lander picked them up at the train station and took them to the spaceport on Ve, the next planet out from Hain. They were rested, tanned, bonded, and ready to go.

One of Sweet Today's hemi-affiliate cousins once removed was on ansible duty in Ve Port. She urged the Shobies to ask the inventors of the churten on Urras and Anarres any questions they had about churten operation. "The purpose of the experimental flight is understanding," she insisted, "and your full intellectual participation is essential. They've been very anxious about that."

Lidi snorted.

"Now for the ritual," said Shan, as they went to the ansible room in the sunward bubble. "They'll explain to the animals what they're going to do and why, and ask them to help."

"The animals don't understand that," Betton said in his cold, angelic treble. "It's just to make the humans feel better."

"The humans understand?" Sweet Today asked.

"We all use each other," Oreth said. "The ritual says: we have no right to do so; therefore, we accept the responsibility for the suffering we cause."

Betton listened and brooded.

Gveter addressed the ansible first and talked to it for half an hour, mostly in Pravic and mathematics. Finally, apologizing, and looking a little unnerved, he invited the others to use the instrument. There was a pause. Lidi activated it, introduced herself, and said, "We have agreed that none of us, except Gveter, has the theoretical background to grasp the principles of the churten."

A scientist twenty-two light-years away responded in Hainish via the rather flat auto-translator voice, but with unmistakable hopefulness, "The churten, in lay terms, may be seen as displacing the virtual field in order to realize relational coherence in terms of the transiliential experientiality."

"Quite," said Lidi.

"As you know, the material effects have been nil, and negative effect on low-intelligence sentients also nil; but there is considered to be a possibility that the participation of high intelligence in the process might affect the displacement in one way or another. And that such displacement would reciprocally affect the participant."

"What has the level of our intelligence got to do with how the churten functions?" Tai asked.

A pause. Their interlocutor was trying to find the words, to accept the responsibility.

"We have been using 'intelligence' as shorthand for the psychic complexity and cultural dependence of our species," said the translator voice at last. "The presence of the transilient as conscious mind non-during transilience is the untested factor."

"But if the process is instantaneous, how can we be conscious of it?" Oreth asked.

"Precisely," said the ansible, and after another pause continued: "As the experimenter is an element of the experiment, so we assume that the transilient may be an element or agent of transilience. This is why we asked for a crew to test the process, rather than one or two volunteers. The psychic interbalance of a bonded social group is a margin of strength against disintegrative or incomprehensible experience, if any such occurs. Also, the separate observations of the group members will mutually interverify."

"Who programs this translator?" Shan snarled in a whisper. "Interverify! Shit!"

Lidi looked around at the others, inviting questions.

"How long will the trip actually take?" Betton asked.

"No long," the translator voice said, then self-corrected: "No time."

Another pause.

"Thank you," said Sweet Today, and the scientist on a planet twenty-two years of time-dilated travel from Ve Port answered, "We are grateful for your generous courage, and our hope is with you."

They went directly from the ansible room to the *Shoby*.

The churten equipment, which was not very space-consuming and the controls of which consisted essentially of an on-off switch, had been installed alongside the Nearly As Fast As Light motivators and controls of an ordinary interstellar ship of the Ekumenical Fleet. The *Shoby* had been built on Hain about four hundred years ago, and was thirty-two years old. Most of its early runs had been exploratory, with a Hainish-Chiffewarian crew. Since in such runs a ship might spend years in orbit in a planetary system, the Hainish and Chiffewarians, feeling that it might as well be lived in rather than endured, had arranged and furnished it like a very large, very comfortable house. Three of its residential modules had been disconnected and left in the hangars on Ve, and still there was more than enough room for a crew of only ten. Tai, Betton, and Shan, new from Terra, and Gveter from Anarres, accustomed to the barracks and the communal austerities of their marginally habitable worlds, stalked about the *Shoby*, disapproving it. "Excremental," Gveter growled. "Luxury!" Tai sneered. Sweet Today, Lidi, and the Gethenians, more used to the amenities of shipboard life, settled right in and made themselves at home. And Gveter and the younger Terrans found it hard to maintain ethical discomfort in the spacious, high-ceilinged, well-furnished, slightly shabby living rooms and bedrooms, studies, high- and low-G gyms, the dining room, library, kitchen, and bridge of the *Shoby*. The carpet in the bridge was a genuine Henyekaulil, soft deep blues and purples woven in the patterns of the constellations of the Hainish sky. There was a large, healthy plantation of Terran bamboo in the meditation gym, part of the ship's self-contained vegetal/respiratory system. The windows of any room could be programmed by the homesick to a view of Abbenay or New Cairo or the beach at Liden, or cleared to look out on the suns nearer and farther and the darkness between the suns.

Rig and Asten discovered that as well as the elevators there was a stately staircase with a curving

banister, leading from the reception hall up to the
library. They slid down the banister shrieking wildly,
until Shan threatened to apply a local gravity field
and force them to slide up it, which they besought
him to do. Betton watched the little ones with a
superior gaze, and took the elevator; but the next
day he slid down the banister, going a good deal
faster than Rig and Asten because he could push off
harder and had greater mass, and nearly broke his
tailbone. It was Betton who organized the tray-slid-
ing races, but Rig generally won them, being small
enough to stay on the tray all the way down the
stairs. None of the children had had any lessons at
the beach, except in swimming and being Shobies;
but while they waited through an unexpected five-
day delay at Ve Port, Gveter did physics with Betton
and math with all three daily in the library, and
they did some history with Shan and Oreth, and
danced with Tai in the low-G gym.

When she danced, Tai became light, free, laughing. Rig and Asten loved her then, and her son
danced with her like a colt, like a kid, awkward and
blissful. Shan often joined them; he was a dark and
elegant dancer, and she would dance with him, but
even then was shy, would not touch. She had been
celibate since Betton's birth. She did not want
Shan's patient, urgent desire, did not want to cope
with it, with him. She would turn from him to Betton, and son and mother would dance wholly
absorbed in the steps, the airy pattern they made
together. Watching them, the afternoon before the
test flight, Sweet Today began to wipe tears from
her eyes, smiling, never saying a word.

"Life is good," said Gveter very seriously to Lidi.

"It'll do," she said.

Oreth, who was just coming out of female kemmer, having thus triggered Karth's male kemmer,
all of which, by coming on unexpectedly early, had

delayed the test flight for these past five days, enjoyable days for all—Oreth watched Rig, whom she had fathered, dance with Asten, whom she had borne, and watched Karth watch them, and said in Karhidish, "Tomorrow . . . " The edge was very sweet.

Anthropologists solemnly agree that we must not attribute "cultural constants" to the human population of any planet; but certain cultural traits or expectations do seem to run deep. Before dinner that last night in port, Shan and Tai appeared in black-and-silver uniforms of the Terran Ekumen, which had cost them—Terra also still had a money economy—a half-year's allowance.

Asten and Rig clamored at once for equal grandeur. Karth and Oreth suggested their party clothes, and Sweet Today brought out silver lace scarves, but Asten sulked, and Rig imitated. The idea of a *uniform*, Asten told them, was that it was the *same*.

"Why?" Oreth inquired.

Old Lidi answered sharply: "So that no one is responsible."

She then went off and changed into a black velvet evening suit that wasn't a uniform but that didn't leave Tai and Shan sticking out like sore thumbs. She had left Terra at age eighteen and never been back nor wanted to, but Tai and Shan were shipmates.

Karth and Oreth got the idea and put on their finest fur-trimmed hiebs, and the children were appeased with their own party clothes plus all of Karth's hereditary and massive gold jewelry. Sweet Today appeared in a pure white robe which she claimed was in fact ultra-violet. Gveter braided his mane. Betton had no uniform, but needed none,

sitting beside his mother at table in a visible glory
of pride.

Meals, sent up from the Port kitchens, were very
good, and this one was superb: a delicate Hainish
iyanwi with all seven sauces, followed by a pudding
flavored with Terran chocolate. A lively evening
ended quietly at the big fireplace in the library. The
logs were fake, of course, but good fakes; no use having a fireplace on a ship and then burning plastic in
it. The neocellulose logs and kindling smelled right,
resisted catching, caught with spits and sparks and
smoke billows, flared up bright. Oreth had laid the
fire, Karth lit it. Everybody gathered round.

"Tell bedtime stories," Rig said.

Oreth told about the Ice Caves of Kerm Land,
how a ship sailed into the great blue sea-cave and
disappeared and was never found by the boats that
entered the caves in search; but seventy years later
that ship was found drifting—not a living soul
aboard nor any sign of what had become of them—
off the coast of Osemyet, a thousand miles overland
from Kerm. . . .

Another story?

Lidi told about the little desert wolf who lost his
wife and went to the land of the dead for her, and
found her there dancing with the dead, and nearly
brought her back to the land of the living, but
spoiled it by trying to touch her before they got all
the way back to life, and she vanished, and he could
never find the way back to the place where the dead
danced, no matter how he looked, and howled, and
cried. . . .

Another story!

Shan told about the boy who sprouted a feather
every time he told a lie, until his commune had to
use him for a duster.

Another!

Gveter told about the winged people called

gluns, who were so stupid that they died out because they kept hitting each other head-on in midair. "They weren't real," he added conscientiously. "Only a story."

Another—No. Bedtime now.

Rig and Asten went round as usual for a goodnight hug, and this time Betton followed them. When he came to Tai he did not stop, for she did not like to be touched; but she put out her hand, drew the child to her, and kissed his cheek. He fled in joy.

"Stories," said Sweet Today. "Ours begins tomorrow, eh?"

A chain of command is easy to describe; a network of response isn't. To those who live by mutual empowerment, "thick" description, complex and open-ended, is normal and comprehensible, but to those whose only model is hierarchic control, such description seems a muddle, a mess, along with what it describes. Who's in charge here? Get rid of all these petty details. How many cooks spoil a soup? Let's get this perfectly clear now. Take me to your leader!

The old navigator was at the NAFAL console, of course, and Gveter at the paltry churten console; Oreth was wired into the AI; Tai, Shan, and Karth were their respective Support, and what Sweet Today did might be called supervising or overseeing if that didn't suggest a hierarchic function. Interseeing, maybe, or subvising. Rig and Asten always naffled (to use Rig's word) in the ship's library, where, during the boring and disorienting experience of travel at near lightspeed, Asten could try to look at pictures or listen to a music tape, and Rig could curl up on and under a certain furry blanket and go to sleep. Betton's crew function during flight was Elder Sib; he stayed with the little ones, provided himself

with a barf bag since he was one of those whom
NAFAL flight made queasy, and focused the intervid
on Lidi and Gveter so he could watch what they did.

So they all knew what they were doing, as
regards NAFAL flight. As regards the churten process, they knew that it was supposed to effectuate
their transilience to a solar system seventeen light-
years from Ve Port without temporal interval; but
nobody, anywhere, knew what they were doing.

So Lidi looked around, like the violinist who
raises her bow to poise the chamber group for the
first chord, a flicker of eye contact, and sent the
Shoby into NAFAL mode, as Gveter, like the cellist
whose bow comes down in that same instant to
ground the chord, sent the *Shoby* into churten mode.
They entered unduration. They churtened. No long,
as the ansible had said.

"What's wrong?" Shan whispered.

"By damn!" said Gveter.

"What?" said Lidi, blinking and shaking her
head.

"That's it," Tai said, flicking readouts.

"That's not A-sixty-whatsit," Lidi said, still blinking.

Sweet Today was gestalting them, all ten at
once, the seven on the bridge and by intervid the
three in the library. Betton had cleared a window,
and the children were looking out at the murky,
brownish convexity that filled half of it. Rig was
holding a dirty, furry blanket. Karth was taking the
electrodes off Oreth's temples, disengaging the AI
link. "There was no interval," Oreth said.

"We aren't anywhere," Lidi said.

"There was no interval," Gveter repeated, scowl-
ing at the console. "That's right."

"Nothing happened," Karth said, skimming
through the AI flight report.

Oreth got up, went to the window, and stood
motionless looking out.

"That's it. M-60-340-nolo," Tai said.

All their words fell dead, had a false sound.

"Well! We did it, Shobies!" said Shan.

Nobody answered.

"Buzz Ve Port on the ansible," Shan said with determined jollity. "Tell 'em we're all here in one piece."

"All where?" Oreth asked.

"Yes, of course," Sweet Today said, but did nothing.

"Right," said Tai, going to the ship's ansible. She opened the field, centered to Ve, and sent a signal. Ships' ansibles worked only in the visual mode; she waited, watching the screen. She resignaled. They were all watching the screen.

"Nothing going through," she said.

Nobody told her to check the centering coordinates; in a network system nobody gets to dump their anxieties that easily. She checked the coordinates. She signaled; rechecked, reset, resignaled; opened the field and centered to Abbenay on Anarres and signaled. The ansible screen was blank.

"Check the—" Shan said, and stopped himself.

"The ansible is not functioning," Tai reported formally to her crew.

"Do you find malfunction?" Sweet Today asked.

"No. Nonfunction."

"We're going back now," said Lidi, still seated at the NAFAL console.

Her words, her tone, shook them, shook them apart.

"No, we're not!" Betton said on the intervid while Oreth said, "Back where?"

Tai, Lidi's Support, moved towards her as if to prevent her from activating the NAFAL drive, but then hastily moved back to the ansible to prevent Gveter from getting access to it. He stopped, taken aback, and said, "Perhaps the churten affected ansible function?"

"*I*'m checking it out," Tai said. "Why should it? Robot-operated ansible transmission functioned in all the test flights."

"Where are the AI reports?" Shan demanded.

"I told you, there are none," Karth answered sharply.

"Oreth was plugged in."

Oreth, still at the window, spoke without turning. "Nothing happened."

Sweet Today came over beside the Gethenian. Oreth looked at her and said, slowly, "Yes. Sweet Today. We cannot . . . do this. I think. I can't think."

Shan had cleared a second window, and stood looking out it. "Ugly," he said.

"What is?" said Lidi.

Gveter said, as if reading from the Ekumenical Atlas, "Thick, stable atmosphere, near the bottom of the temperature window for life. Micro-organisms. Bacterial clouds, bacterial reefs."

"Germ stew," Shan said. "Lovely place to send us."

"So that if we arrived as a neutron bomb or a black hole event we'd only take bacteria with us," Tai said. "But we didn't."

"Didn't what?" said Lidi.

"Didn't arrive?" Karth asked.

"Hey," Betton said, "is everybody going to stay on the bridge?"

"I want to come there," said Rig's little pipe, and then Asten's voice, clear but shaky, "Maba, I'd like to go back to Liden now."

"Come on," Karth said, and went to meet the children. Oreth did not turn from the window, even when Asten came close and took Oreth's hand.

"What are you looking at, Maba?"

"The planet, Asten."

"What planet?"

Oreth looked at the child then.

"There isn't anything," Asten said.

"That brown color—that's the surface, the atmosphere of a planet."

"There isn't any brown color. There isn't *anything*. I want to go back to Liden. You said we could when we were done with the test."

Oreth looked around, at last, at the others.

"Perception variation," Gveter said.

"I think," Tai said, "that we must establish that we are—that we got here—and then get here."

"You mean, go back," Betton said.

"The readings are perfectly clear," Lidi said, holding on to the rim of her seat with both hands and speaking very distinctly. "Every coordinate in order. That's M-60-Etcetera down there. What more do you want? Bacteria samples?"

"Yes," Tai said. "Instrument function's been affected, so we can't rely on instrumental records."

"Oh, shitsake!" said Lidi. "What a farce! All right. Suit up, go down, get some goo, and then let's get out. Go home. By NAFAL."

"By NAFAL?" Shan and Tai echoed, and Gveter said, "But we would spend seventeen years, Ve time, and no ansible to explain why."

"Why, Lidi?" Sweet Today asked.

Lidi stared at the Hainishwoman. "You want to churten again?" she demanded, raucous. She looked round at them all. "Are you people made of stone?" Her face was ashy, crumpled, shrunken. "It doesn't bother you, seeing through the walls?"

No one spoke, until Shan said cautiously, "How do you mean?"

"I can see the stars through the walls!" She stared round at them again, pointing at the carpet with its woven constellations. "You can't?" When no one answered, her jaw trembled in a little spasm, and she said, "All right. All right. I'm off duty. Sorry. Be in my room." She stood up. "Maybe you should lock me in," she said.

"Nonsense," said Sweet Today.

"If I fall through . . . " Lidi began, and did not finish. She walked to the door, stiffly and cautiously, as if through a thick fog. She said something they did not understand, "Cause," or perhaps, "Gauze."

Sweet Today followed her.

"I can see the stars too!" Rig announced.

"Hush," Karth said, putting an arm around the child.

"I can! I can see all the stars everywhere. And I can see Ve Port. And I can see anything I want!"

"Yes, of course, but hush now," the mother murmured, at which the child pulled free, stamped, and shrilled, "I can! I can too! I can see *everything!* And Asten can't! And there *is* a planet, there is too! No, don't hold me! Don't! Let me go!"

Grim, Karth carried the screaming child off to their quarters. Asten turned around to yell after Rig, "There is *not* any planet! You're just making it up!"

Grim, Oreth said, "Go to our room, please, Asten."

Asten burst into tears and obeyed. Oreth, with a glance of apology to the others, followed the short, weeping figure across the bridge and out into the corridor.

The four remaining on the bridge stood silent.

"Canaries," Shan said.

"Khallucinations?" Gveter proposed, subdued. "An effect of the churten on extrasensitive organisms— maybe?"

Tai nodded.

"Then is the ansible not functioning, or are we hallucinating nonfunction?" Shan asked after a pause.

Gveter went to the ansible; this time Tai walked away from it, leaving it to him. "I want to go down," she said.

"No reason not to, I suppose," Shan said unenthusiastically.

"Khwat reason to?" Gveter asked over his shoulder.

"It's what we're here for, isn't it? It's what we volunteered to do, isn't it? To test instantaneous—transilience—prove that it worked, that we are here! With the ansible out, it'll be seventeen years before Ve gets our radio signal!"

"We can just churten back to Ve and *tell* them," Shan said. "If we did that now, we'd have been . . . here . . . about eight minutes."

"Tell them—tell them what? What kind of evidence is that?"

"Anecdotal," said Sweet Today, who had come back quietly to the bridge; she moved like a big sailing ship, imposingly silent.

"Is Lidi all right?" Shan asked.

"No," Sweet Today answered. She sat down where Lidi had sat, at the NAFAL console.

"I ask a consensus about going down onplanet," Tai said.

"I'll ask the others," Gveter said, and went out, returning presently with Karth. "Go down, if you want," the Gethenian said. "Oreth's staying with the children for a bit. They are—We are extremely disoriented."

"I will come down," Gveter said.

"Can I come?" Betton asked, almost in a whisper, not raising his eyes to any adult face.

"No," Tai said, as Gveter said, "Yes."

Betton looked at his mother, one quick glance.

"Khwy not?" Gveter asked her.

"We don't know the risks."

"The planet was surveyed."

"By robot ships—"

"We'll wear suits." Gveter was honestly puzzled.

"I don't want the responsibility," Tai said through her teeth.

"Khwy is it yours?" Gveter asked, more puzzled still. "We all share it; Betton is crew. I don't understand."

"I know you don't understand," Tai said, turned her back on them both, and went out. The man and the boy stood staring, Gveter after Tai, Betton at the carpet.

"I'm sorry," Betton said.

"Not to be," Gveter told him.

"What is . . . what is going on?" Shan asked in an overcontrolled voice. "Why are we—We keep crossing, we keep—coming and going—"

"Confusion due to the churten experience," Gveter said.

Sweet Today turned from the console. "I have sent a distress signal," she said. "I am unable to operate the NAFAL system. The radio—" She cleared her throat. "Radio function seems erratic."

There was a pause.

"This is not happening," Shan said, or Oreth said, but Oreth had stayed with the children in another part of the ship, so it could not have been Oreth who said, "This is not happening," it must have been Shan.

A chain of cause and effect is an easy thing to describe; a cessation of cause and effect is not. To those who live in time, sequence is the norm, the only model, and simultaneity seems a muddle, a mess, a hopeless confusion, and the description of that confusion hopelessly confusing. As the members of the crew network no longer perceived the network steadily and were unable to communicate their perceptions, an individual perception is the only clue to follow through the labyrinth of their dislocation. Gveter perceived himself as being on the bridge with Shan, Sweet Today, Betton, Karth, and Tai. He perceived himself as methodically checking out the ship's systems. The NAFAL he found dead, the radio functioning in erratic bursts, the internal electrical and mechanical systems of the ship all in order. He sent out a lander unmanned and brought it back, and perceived it as functioning normally. He perceived himself discussing with Tai her determination to go down onplanet. Since he admitted his unwillingness to trust any instrumental reading on the ship, he had to admit her point that only material evidence would show that they had actually arrived at their destination, M-60-340-nolo. If they were going to have to spend the next seventeen years traveling back to Ve in real time, it would be nice to have something to show for it, even if only a handful of slime.

He perceived this discussion as perfectly rational.

It was, however, interrupted by outbursts of egoizing not characteristic of the crew.

"If you're going, go!" Shan said.

"Don't give me orders," Tai said.

"Somebody's got to stay in control here," Shan said.

"Not the men!" Tai said.

"Not the Terrans," Karth said. "Have you people no self-respect?"

"Stress," Gveter said. "Come on, Tai, Betton, all right, let's go, all right?"

In the lander, everything was clear to Gveter. One thing happened after another just as it should. Lander operation is very simple, and he asked Betton to take them down. The boy did so. Tai sat, tense and compact as always, her strong fists clenched on her knees. Betton managed the little ship with aplomb, and sat back, tense also, but dignified: "We're down," he said.

"No, we're not," Tai said.

"It—it says contact," Betton said, losing his assurance.

"An excellent landing," Gveter said. "Never even felt it." He was running the usual tests. Everything was in order. Outside the lander ports pressed a brownish darkness, a gloom. When Betton put on the outside lights the atmosphere, like a dark fog, diffused the light into a useless glare.

"Tests all tally with survey reports," Gveter said. "Will you go out, Tai, or use the servos?"

"Out," she said.

"Out," Betton echoed.

Gveter, assuming the formal crew role of Support, which one of them would have assumed if he had been going out, assisted them to lock their helmets and decontaminate their suits; he opened the hatch series for them, and watched them on the vid and from the port as they climbed down from the outer hatch. Betton went first. His slight figure, elongated by the whitish suit, was luminous in the weak glare of the lights. He walked a few steps from the ship, turned, and waited. Tai was stepping off the ladder. She seemed to grow very short—did she kneel down? Gveter looked from the port to the vid screen and back. She was shrinking? sinking—she must be sinking into the surface—which could not be solid, then, but bog, or some suspension like quicksand—but Betton had walked on it and was walking back to her, two steps, three steps, on the ground which Gveter could not see clearly but which must be solid, and which must be holding Betton up because he was lighter—but no, Tai must have stepped into a hole, a trench of some kind, for he could see her only from the waist up now, her legs hidden in the dark bog or fog, but she was moving, moving quickly, going right away from the lander and from Betton.

"Bring them back," Shan said, and Gveter said on the suit intercom, "Please return to the lander, Betton and Tai." Betton at once started up the ladder, then turned to look for his mother. A dim blotch that might be her helmet showed in the brown gloom, almost beyond the suffusion of light from the lander.

"Please come in, Betton. Please return, Tai."

The whitish suit flickered up the ladder, while Betton's voice in the intercom pleaded, "Tai—Tai, come back—Gveter, should I go after her?"

"No. Tai, please return at once to lander."

The boy's crew-integrity held; he came up into the lander and watched from the outer hatch, as Gveter watched from the port. The vid had lost her. The pallid blotch sank into the formless murk.

Gveter perceived that the instruments recorded that the lander had sunk 3.2 meters since contact with planet surface and was continuing to sink at an increasing rate.

"What is the surface, Betton?"

"Like muddy ground—Where is she?"

"Please return at once, Tai!"

"Please return to *Shoby*, Lander One and all crew," said the ship intercom; it was Tai's voice. "This is Tai," it said. "Please return at once to ship, lander and all crew."

"Stay in suit, in decon, please, Betton," Gveter said. "I'm sealing the hatch."

"But—All right," said the boy's voice.

Gveter took the lander up, decontaminating it and Betton's suit on the way. He perceived that Betton and Shan came with him through the hatch series into the *Shoby* and along the halls to the bridge, and that Karth, Sweet Today, Shan, and Tai were on the bridge.

Betton ran to his mother and stopped; he did not put out his hands to her. His face was immobile, as if made of wax or wood.

"Were you frightened?" she asked. "What happened down there?" And she looked to Gveter for an explanation.

Gveter perceived nothing. Unduring a nonperiod

of no long, he perceived nothing was had happening happened that had not happened. Lost, he
groped, lost, he found the word, the word that
saved—"You—" he said, his tongue thick, dumb—
"You called us."

It seemed that she denied, but it did not matter.
What mattered? Shan was talking. Shan could tell.
"Nobody called, Gveter," he said. "You and Betton
went out, I was Support; when I realized I couldn't
get the lander stable, that there's something funny
about that surface, I called you back into the lander,
and we came up."

All Gveter could say was, "Insubstantial . . . "

"But Tai came—" Betton began, and stopped.
Gveter perceived that the boy moved away from his
mother's denying touch. What mattered?

"Nobody went down," Sweet Today said. After a
silence and before it, she said, "There is no down to
go to."

Gveter tried to find another word, but there was
none. He perceived outside the main port a brownish, murky convexity, through which, as he looked
intently, he saw small stars shining.

He found a word then, the wrong word. "Lost,"
he said, and speaking perceived how the ship's
lights dimmed slowly into a brownish murk, faded,
darkened, were gone, while all the soft hum and
busyness of the ship's systems died away into the
real silence that was always there. But there was
nothing there. Nothing had happened. We are at Ve
Port! he tried with all his will to say; but there was
no saying.

The suns burn through my flesh, Lidi said.

I am the suns, said Sweet Today. Not I, all is.

Don't breathe! cried Oreth.

It is death, Shan said. What I feared, is: nothing.

Nothing, they said.

Unbreathing, the ghosts flitted, shifted, in the

ghost shell of a cold, dark hull floating near a world of brown fog, an unreal planet. They spoke, but there were no voices. There is no sound in vacuum, nor in nontime.

In her cabined solitude, Lidi felt the gravity lighten to the half-G of the ship's core-mass; she saw them, the nearer and the farther suns, burn through the dark gauze of the walls and hulls and the bedding and her body. The brightest, the sun of this system, floated directly under her navel. She did not know its name.

I am the darkness between the suns, one said.

I am nothing, one said.

I am you, one said.

You—one said—You—

And breathed, and reached out, and spoke: "Listen!" Crying out to the other, to the others, "Listen!"

"We have always known this. This is where we have always been, will always be, at the hearth, at the center. There is nothing to be afraid of, after all."

"I can't breathe," one said.

"I am not breathing," one said.

"There is nothing to breathe," one said.

"You are, you are breathing, please breathe!" said another.

"We're here, at the hearth," said another.

Oreth had laid the fire, Karth lit it. As it caught they both said softly, in Karhidish, "Praise also the light, and creation unfinished."

The fire caught with spark-spits, crackles, sudden flares. It did not go out. It burned. The others grouped round.

They were nowhere, but they were nowhere together; the ship was dead, but they were in the ship. A dead ship cools off fairly quickly, but not immediately. Close the doors, come in by the fire; keep the cold night out, before we go to bed.

Karth went with Rig to persuade Lidi from her

starry vault. The navigator would not get up. "It's my fault," she said.

"Don't egoize," Karth said mildly. "How could it be?"

"I don't know. I want to stay here," Lidi muttered. Then Karth begged her: "Oh, Lidi, not alone!"

"How else?" the old woman asked, coldly.

But she was ashamed of herself, then, and ashamed of her guilt trip, and growled, "Oh, all right." She heaved herself up and wrapped a blanket around her body and followed Karth and Rig. The child carried a little biolume; it glowed in the black corridors, just as the plants of the aerobic tanks lived on, metabolizing, making an air to breathe, for a while. The light moved before her like a star among the stars through darkness to the room full of books, where the fire burned in the stone hearth. "Hello, children," Lidi said. "What are we doing here?"

"Telling stories," Sweet Today replied.

Shan had a little voice-recorder notebook in his hand.

"Does it work?" Lidi inquired.

"Seems to. We thought we'd tell . . . what happened," Shan said, squinting the narrow black eyes in his narrow black face at the firelight. "Each of us. What we—what it seemed like, seems like, to us. So that . . . "

"As a record, yes. In case . . . How funny that it works, though, your notebook. When nothing else does."

"It's voice-activated," Shan said absently. "So. Go on, Gveter."

Gveter finished telling his version of the expedition to the planet's surface. "We didn't even bring back samples," he ended. "I never thought of them."

"Shan went with you, not me," Tai said.

"You did go, and I did," the boy said with a certainty that stopped her. "And we did go outside. And Shan and Gveter were Support, in the lander. And I took samples. They're in the Stasis closet."

"I don't know if Shan was in the lander or not," Gveter said, rubbing his forehead painfully.

"Where would the lander have gone?" Shan said. "Nothing is out there—we're nowhere—outside time, is all I can think—But when one of you tells how they saw it, it seems as if it was that way, but then the next one changes the story, and I . . . "

Oreth shivered, drawing closer to the fire.

"I never believed this damn thing would work," said Lidi, bearlike in the dark cave of her blanket.

"Not understanding it was the trouble," Karth said. "None of us understood how it would work, not even Gveter. Isn't that true?"

"Yes," Gveter said.

"So that if our psychic interaction with it affected the process—"

"Or *is* the process," said Sweet Today, "so far as we're concerned."

"Do you mean," Lidi said in a tone of deep existential disgust, "that we have to *believe* in it to make it work?"

"You have to believe in yourself in order to act, don't you?" Tai said.

"No," the navigator said. "Absolutely not. I don't believe in myself. I *know* some things. Enough to go on."

"An analogy," Gveter offered. "The effective action of a crew depends on the members perceiving themselves as a crew—you could call it believing in the crew, or just *being* it—Right? So, maybe, to churten, we—we conscious ones—maybe it depends on our consciously perceiving ourselves as . . . as transilient—as being in the other place—the destination?"

"We lost our crewness, certainly, for a—Are there whiles?" Karth said. "We fell apart."

"We lost the thread," Shan said.

"Lost," Oreth said meditatively, laying another massive, half-weightless log on the fire, volleying sparks up into the chimney, slow stars.

"We lost—what?" Sweet Today asked.

No one answered for a while.

"When I can see the sun through the carpet . . . " Lidi said.

"So can I," Betton said, very low.

"I can see Ve Port," said Rig. "And everything. I can tell you what I can see. I can see Liden if I look. And my room on the *Oneblin*. And—"

"First, Rig," said Sweet Today, "tell us what happened."

"All right," Rig said agreeably. "Hold on to me harder, maba, I start floating. Well, we went to the liberry, me and Asten and Betton, and Betton was Elder Sib, and the adults were on the bridge, and I was going to go to sleep like I do when we naffle-fly, but before I even lay down there was the brown planet and Ve Port and both the suns and everywhere else, and you could see through everything, but Asten couldn't. But I can."

"We never went *anywhere*," Asten said. "Rig tells stories all the time."

"We all tell stories all the time, Asten," Karth said.

"Not dumb ones like Rig's!"

"Even dumber," said Oreth. "What we need . . . What we need is . . . "

"We need to know," Shan said, "what transilience is, and we don't, because we never did it before, nobody ever did it before."

"Not in the flesh," said Lidi.

"We need to know what's—real—what happened, *whether* anything happened—" Tai gestured at the cave of firelight around them and the dark beyond it. "Where are we? Are we here? Where is here? What's the story?"

"We have to tell it," Sweet Today said. "Recount it. Relate it. . . . Like Rig. Asten, how does a story begin?"

"A thousand winters ago, a thousand miles away," the child said; and Shan murmured, "Once upon a time . . . "

"There was a ship called the *Shoby*," said Sweet Today, "on a test flight, trying out the churten, with a crew of ten.

"Their names were Rig, Asten, Betton, Karth, Oreth, Lidi, Tai, Shan, Gveter, and Sweet Today. And they related their story, each one and together. . . ."

There was silence, the silence that was always there, except for the stir and crackle of the fire and the small sounds of their breathing, their movements, until one of them spoke at last, telling the story.

"The boy and his mother," said the light, pure voice, "were the first human beings ever to set foot on that world."

Again the silence; and again a voice.

"Although she wished . . . she realized that she really hoped the thing wouldn't work, because it would make her skills, her whole life, obsolete . . . all the same she really wanted to learn how to use it, too, if she could, if she wasn't too old to learn. . . ."

A long, softly throbbing pause, and another voice.

"They went from world to world, and each time they lost the world they left, lost it in time dilation, their friends getting old and dying while they were in NAFAL flight. If there were a way to live in one's own time, and yet move among the worlds, they wanted to try it. . . ."

"Staking everything on it," the next voice took up the story, "because nothing works except what we give our souls to, nothing's safe except what we put at risk."

A while, a little while; and a voice.

"It was like a game. It was like we were still in the *Shoby* at Ve Port just waiting before we went into NAFAL flight. But it was like we were at the brown planet too. At the same time. And one of them was just pretend, and the other one wasn't, but I didn't know which. So it was like when you pretend in a game. But I didn't want to play. I didn't know how."

Another voice.

"If the churten principle were proved to be applicable to actual transilience of living, conscious beings, it would be a great event in the mind of his people—for all people. A new understanding. A new partnership. A new way of being in the universe. A wider freedom. . . . He wanted that very much. He wanted to be one of the crew that first formed that partnership, the first people to be able to think this thought, and to . . . to relate it. But also he was afraid of it. Maybe it wasn't a true relation, maybe false, maybe only a dream. He didn't know."

It was not so cold, so dark, at their backs, as they sat round the fire. Was it the waves of Liden, hushing on the sand?

Another voice.

"She thought a lot about her people, too. About guilt, and expiation, and sacrifice. She wanted a lot to be on this flight that might give people—more freedom. But it was different from what she thought it would be. What happened—What *happened* wasn't what mattered. What mattered was that she came to be with people who gave *her* freedom. Without guilt. She wanted to stay with them, to be crew with them. . . . And with her son. Who was the first human being to set foot on an unknown world."

A long silence; but not deep, only as deep as the soft drum of the ship's systems, steady and unconscious as the circulation of the blood.

Another voice.

"They were thoughts in the mind; what else had they ever been? So they could be in Ve and at the brown planet, and desiring flesh and entire spirit, and illusion and reality, all at once, as they'd always been. When he remembered this, his confusion and fear ceased, for he knew that they couldn't be lost."

"They got lost. But they found the way," said another voice, soft above the hum and hushing of the ship's systems, in the warm fresh air and light inside the solid walls and hulls.

Only nine voices had spoken, and they looked for the tenth; but the tenth had gone to sleep, thumb in mouth.

"That story was told and is yet to be told," the mother said. "Go on. I'll churten here with Rig."

They left those two by the fire, and went to the bridge, and then to the hatches to invite on board a crowd of anxious scientists, engineers, and officials of Ve Port and the Ekumen, whose instruments had been assuring them that the *Shoby* had vanished, forty-four minutes ago, into non-existence, into silence. "What happened?" they asked. "What happened?" And the Shobies looked at one another and said, "Well, it's quite a story. . . ."

DANCING TO GANAM

"Power is the great drumming," Aketa said. "The thunder. The noise of the waterfall that makes the electricity. It fills you till there's no room for anything else."

Ket poured a few drops of water onto the ground, murmuring, "Drink, traveler." She sprinkled pollen meal over the ground, murmuring, "Eat, traveler." She looked up at Iyananam, the mountain of power. "Maybe he only listened to the thunder, and couldn't hear anything else," she said. "Do you think he knew what he was doing?"

"I think he knew what he was doing," Aketa said.

Since the successful though problematic transilience of the *Shoby* to and from a nasty little planet called M-60-340-nolo, a whole wing of Ve Port had been given over to churten technology. The originators of churten theory on Anarres and the engineers of transilience on Urras communicated constantly by ansible with the theorists and engineers on Ve, who set up experiments and investigations designed to find out what, in fact, happened when a ship and its crew went from one place in the universe to another without taking any time at all to do so. "You cannot say 'went,' you cannot say 'happened,'" the Cetians chided. "It is here not there in one moment and in that same moment it is there not here. The non-interval is called, in our language, churten."

Interlocking with these circles of Cetian temporal-ists were circles of Hainish psychologists, investigating and arguing about what, in fact, happened when intel-ligent life-forms experienced the churten. "You cannot say 'in fact,' you cannot say 'experienced,'" they chided. "The reality point of 'arrival' for a churten crew is obtained by mutual perception-comparison and adjustment, so that for thinking beings construc-tion of event is essential to effective transilience," and so on, and on, for the Hainish have been talking for a million years and have never got tired of it. But they are also fond of listening, and they listened to what the crew of the *Shoby* had to tell them. And when Commander Dalzul arrived, they listened to him.

"You have to send one man alone," he said. "The problem is interference. There were ten people on the *Shoby*. Send one man. Send me."

"You ought to go with Shan," Betton said.

His mother shook her head.

"It's dumb not to go!"

"If they don't want you, they don't get me," she said.

The boy knew better than to hug her, or say any-thing much. But he did something he seldom did: he made a joke. "You'd be back in no time," he said.

"Oh, get along," Tai said.

* * *

Shan knew that the Hainish did not wear uniforms and did not use status indicators such as "Commander." But he put on his black-and-silver uniform of the Terran Ekumen to meet Commander Dalzul.

Born in the barracks of Alberta in the earliest years of Terra's membership in the Ekumen, Dalzul took a degree in temporal physics at the University of A-Io on Urras and trained with the Stabiles on Hain before returning to his native planet as a Mobile of the Ekumen of the Worlds. During the sixty-seven years of his near-lightspeed journey, a troublesome religious movement escalated into the horrors of the Unist Revolution. Dalzul got the situation under control within months, by a combination of acumen and tactics that won him the respect of those he worked for, and the worship of those he had worked against—for the Unist Fathers decided he was God. The worldwide slaughter of unbelievers devolved into a worldwide novena of adoration of the New Manifestation, before devolving further into schisms and sects intent mainly on killing one another. Dalzul had defused the worst resurgence of theocratic violence since the Time of Pollution. He had acted with grace, with wit, with patience, reliability, resilience, trickiness, and good humor, with all the means the Ekumen most honored.

As he could not work on Terra, being prey to deification, he was given obscure but significant tasks on obscure but significant planets; one of them was Orint, the only world from which the Ekumen had yet withdrawn. They did so on Dalzul's advice, shortly before the Orintians destroyed sentient life on their world by the use of pathogens in war. Dalzul had foretold the event with terrible and compassionate accuracy. He had set up the secret, last-minute rescue of a few thousand children whose parents were willing to let them go; Dalzul's Children, these last of the Orintians were called.

Shan knew that heroes were phenomena of primitive cultures; but Terra's culture was primitive, and Dalzul was his hero.

Tai read the message from Ve Port with disbelief. "What kind of crew is that?" she said. "Who asks parents to leave their kid?"

Then she looked up at Shan, and saw his face.

"It's Dalzul," he said. "He wants us. In his crew."

"Go," Tai said.

He argued, of course, but Tai was on the hero's side. He went. And for the reception at which he was to meet Dalzul, he wore the black uniform with the silver thread down the sleeves and the one silver circle over the heart.

The commander wore the same uniform. When he saw him Shan's heart leaped and thudded. Inevitably, Dalzul was shorter than Shan had imagined him: he was not three meters tall. But otherwise he was as he should be, erect and lithe, the long, light hair going grey pulled back from a magnificent, vivid face, the eyes as clear as water. Shan had not realized how white-skinned Dalzul was, but the deformity or atavism was minor and could even be seen as having its own beauty. Dalzul's voice was warm and quiet; he laughed as he talked to a group of excited Anarresti. He saw Shan, turned, came straight to him. "At last! You're Shan, I'm Dalzul, we're shipmates. I am truly sorry your partner couldn't be one of us. But her replacements are old friends of yours, I think—Forest and Riel."

Shan was delighted to see the two familiar faces, Forest's an obsidian knife with watchful eyes, Riel's round and shining as a copper sun. He had been in training on Ollul with them. They greeted him with equal pleasure. "This is wonderful," he said, and then, "So we're all Terrans?"—a stupid

question, since the fact was obvious; but the Ekumen generally favored mixing cultures in a crew.

"Come on out of this," Dalzul said, "and I'll
explain." He signaled a mezklete, which trotted
over, proudly pushing a little cart laden with drinks
and food. They filled trays, thanked the mezklete,
and found themselves a deep windowseat well away
from the noisy throng. There they sat and ate and
drank and talked and listened. Dalzul did not try to
hide his passionate conviction that he was on the
right track to solve the "churten problem."

"I've gone out twice alone," he said. He lowered
his voice slightly as he spoke, and Shan began naively,
"Without—?" and stopped.

Dalzul grinned. "No, no. With the permission of
the Churten Research Group. But not really with
their blessing. That's why I tend to whisper and look
over my shoulder. There are still some CRG people
here who make me feel as if I'd stolen their ship—
scoffed at their theories—violated their shifgrethor—
peed on their shoes—even after the ship and I round-
tripped with no churten problems, no perceptual
dissonances at all."

"Where?" Forest asked, blade-sharp face intent.

"First trip, inside this system, from Ve to Hain
and back. A bus trip. Everything known, expectable.
It was absolutely without incident—as expected. I'm
here: I'm there. I leave the ship to check in with the
Stabiles, get back in the ship, and I'm here. Hey
presto! It is magic, you know. And yet it seems so
natural. Where one is, one is. Did you feel that,
Shan?"

The clear eyes were amazing in their intensity.
It was like being looked at by lightning. Shan wanted to be able to agree, but had to stammer, "I—we,
you know, we had some trouble deciding where we
were."

"I think that that's unnecessary, that confusion.

Transilience is a non-experience. I think that normally, *nothing happens*. Literally nothing. Extraneous events got mixed into it in the *Shoby* experiment— your interval was queered. This time, I think we can have a non-experience." He looked at Forest and Riel and laughed. "You'll not-see what I don't mean," he said. "Anyhow, after the bus trip, I hung about annoying them persistently until Gvonesh agreed to let me do a solo exploratory."

The mezklete bustled up to them, pushing its little cart with its furry paws. Mezkletes love parties, love to give food, love to serve drinks and watch their humans get weird. It stayed about hopefully for a while to see if they would get weird, then bustled back to the Anarresti theorists, who were always weird.

"An exploratory—a first contact?"

Dalzul nodded. His strength and unconscious dignity were daunting, and yet his delight, his simple glee, in what he had done was irresistible. Shan had met brilliant people and wise people, but never one whose energy shone so bright, so clear, so vulnerable.

"We chose a distant one. G-14-214-yomo; it was Tadkla on the maps of the Expansion; the people I met there call it Ganam. A preliminary Ekumen mission is actually on its way there at NAFAL speed. Left Ollul eight years ago, and will get there thirteen years from herenow. Of course there was no way to communicate with them while they're in transit, to tell them I was going to be there ahead of them. The CRG thought it a good idea that somebody would be dropping in after thirteen years. In case I didn't report back, maybe they could find out what happened. But it looks now as if the mission will arrive to find Ganam already a member of the Ekumen!" He looked at them all, alight with passion and intention. "You know, churten is going to change everything. When transilience replaces space travel—all travel—when there is no distance between worlds—when we control interval—I keep trying to imagine, to understand what it will mean, to the Ekumen, to us. We'll be able to make the household of humankind truly one house, one place. But then it goes still deeper! In transilience what we do is to rejoin, restore the primal moment, the beat that is the rhythm. . . . To rejoin unity. To escape time. To use eternity! You've been there, Shan—you felt what I'm trying to say?"

"I don't know," Shan said, "yes—"

"Do you want to see the tape of my trip?" Dalzul asked abruptly, his eyes shining with a flicker of mischief. "I brought a handview."

"Yes!" Forest and Riel said, and they crowded in around him in the windowseat like a bunch of conspirators. The mezklete tried in vain to see what they were doing, but was too short, even when it got up on its cart.

While he programmed the little viewer, Dalzul told them briefly about Ganam. One of the outermost seedings of the Hainish Expansion, the world had been lost from the human community for five hundred millennia; nothing was known about it except that it might have a population descended from human ancestors. If it did, the Ekumenical ship on its way to it would in the normal way have observed from orbit for a long time before sending down a few observers, to hide, or to pass if possible, or to reveal their mission if necessary, while gathering information, learning languages and customs, and so on—a process usually of many years. All this had been short-circuited by the unpredictability of the new technology. Dalzul's small ship had come out of churten not in the stratosphere as intended, but in the atmosphere, about a hundred meters above the ground.

"I didn't have the chance to make an unobtrusive

entrance on the scene," he said. The audiovisual
record his ship's instruments had made came up on
the little screen as he spoke. They saw the grey
plains of Ve Port dropping away as the ship left the
planet. "Now," Dalzul said, and in one instant they
saw the stars blaze in black space and the yellow
walls and orange roofs of a city, the blaze of sunlight
on a canal.

"You see?" Dalzul murmured. "Nothing happens."

The city tilted and settled, sunny streets and
squares full of people, all of them looking up and
pointing, unmistakably shouting, "Look! Look!"

"Decided I might as well accept the situation,"
Dalzul said. Trees and grass rose up around the ship
as he brought it on down. People were already hurrying out of the city, human people: terra-
cotta-colored, rather massively built, with broad
faces, bare-armed, barefoot, wearing kilts and gilets
in splendid colors, men with great gold earrings,
headdresses of basketry, gold wire, feather plumes.

"The Gaman," Dalzul said. "The people of
Ganam. . . . Grand, aren't they? And they don't waste
time. They were there within half an hour—there,
that's Ket, see her, that stunning woman?—Since the
ship was obviously fairly alarming, I decided that the
first point to make was my defenselessness."

They saw what he meant, as the ship's camera
recorded his exit. He walked slowly out on the grass
and stood still, facing the gathering crowd. He was
naked. Unarmed, unclothed, alone, he stood there,
the fierce sun bright on his white skin and silvery
hair, his hands held wide and open in the gesture of
offering.

The pause was very long. Talk and exclamation
among the Gaman died out as people came near the
front of the crowd. Dalzul, in the center of the camera's field, stood easily, motionless. Then—Shan
drew breath sharply as he watched—a woman came

forward towards him. She was tall and strongly
built, with round arms, black eyes above high
cheekbones. Her hair was braided with gold into a
coronet on her head. She stood before Dalzul and
spoke, her voice clear and full. The words sounded
like poetry, like ritual questions, Shan thought.
Dalzul responded by bringing his hands toward his
heart, then opening them again wide, palm up.

The woman gazed at him a while, then spoke
one resonant word. Slowly, with a grave formality,
she slipped the dark red gilet from her breasts and
shoulders, untied her kilt and dropped it aside with
a splendid, conscious gesture, and stood naked
before the naked man.

She reached out her hand. Dalzul took it.

They walked away from the ship, towards the
city. The crowd closed in behind them and followed
them, still quiet, without haste or confusion, as if
performing actions they had performed before.

A few people, mostly adolescents, stayed behind,
looking at the ship, daring each other to come closer,
curious, cautious, but not frightened.

Dalzul stopped the tape.

"You see," he said to Shan, "the difference?"

Shan, awed, did not speak.

"What the *Shoby*'s crew discovered," Dalzul said
to the three of them, "is that individual experiences
of transilience can be made coherent only by a con-
certed effort. An effort to synchronize—to entrain.
When they realized that, they were able to pull out
of an increasingly dangerously fragmented perception of where they were and what was happening.
Right, Shan?"

"They call it the chaos experience now," Shan
said, subdued by the memory of it, and by the difference of Dalzul's experience.

"The temporalists and psychologists have sweated
a lot of theory out of the *Shoby* trip," Dalzul said.

"My reading of it is pitifully simple: that a great deal of the perceptual dissonance, the anguish and incoherence, was an effect of the disparity of the *Shoby* crew. No matter how well you had crew-bonded, Shan, you were ten people from four worlds—four different cultures—two very old women, and three young children! If the answer to coherent transilience is entrainment, functioning in rhythm, then we've got to make entrainment easy. That you achieved it at all was miraculous. The simplest way to achieve it, of course, is to bypass it: to go alone."

"Then how do you get a cross-check on the experience?" Forest said.

"You just saw it: the ship's record of the landing."

"But our instruments on the *Shoby* went out, or were totally erratic," Shan said. "The readings are as incoherent as our perceptions were."

"Exactly! You and the instruments were all in one entrainment field, fouling each other up. But when just two or three of you went down onto the planet's surface, things were better: the lander functioned perfectly, and its tapes of the surface are clear. Although very ugly."

Shan laughed. "Ugly, yes. A sort of shit-planet. But, Commander, even on the tapes it never is clear who actually went out onto the surface. And that was one of the most chaotic parts of the whole experience. I went down with Gveter and Betton. The surface under the ship was unstable, so I called them back to the lander and we went back up to the ship. That all seems coherent. But Gveter's perception was that he went down with Betton and Tai, not me, heard Tai call him from the ship, and came back with Betton and me. As for Betton, he went down with Tai and me. He saw his mother walk away from the lander, ignore the order to return, and be left on the surface. Gveter saw that too. They came back without her and found her waiting for them on the bridge. Tai herself has no memory of going down in the lander. Those four stories are all our evidence. They seem to be equally true, equally untrue. And the tapes don't help—don't show who was in the suits. They all look alike in that shit soup on the surface."

"That's it—exactly—" Dalzul said, leaning forward, his face alight. "That murk, that shit, that chaos you saw, which the cameras in your field saw—Think of the difference between that and the tapes we just watched! Sunlight, vivid faces, bright colors, everything brilliant, clear—Because there was no interference, Shan. The Cetians say that in the churten field there is nothing but the deep rhythms, the vibration of the ultimate wave-particles. Transilience is a function of the rhythm that makes being. According to Cetian spiritual physics, it's access to that rhythm which allows the individual to participate in eternity and ubiquity. My extrapolation from that is that individuals in transilience have to be in nearly perfect synchrony to arrive at the same place with a harmonious—that is, an accurate—perception of it. My intuition, as far as we've tested it, has been confirmed: one person can churten sanely. Until we learn what we're doing, ten persons will inevitably experience chaos, or worse."

"And four persons?" Forest inquired, drily.

"—are the control," said Dalzul. "Frankly, I'd rather have started out by going on more solos, or with one companion at most. But our friends from Anarres, as you know, are very distrustful of what they call egoizing. To them, morality isn't accessible to individuals, only to groups. Also, they say, maybe something else went wrong on the *Shoby* experiment, maybe a group can churten just as well as one person, how do we know till we try? So I compromised. I said, send me with two or three highly compatible and highly motivated companions. Send us back to Ganam and let's see what we see!"

"'Motivated' is inadequate," Shan said. "I am committed. I belong to this crew."

Riel was nodding; Forest, wary and saturnine, said only, "Are we going to practice entrainment, Commander?"

"As long as you like," Dalzul said. "But there are things more important than practice. Do you sing, Forest, or play an instrument?"

"I can sing," Forest said, and Riel and Shan nodded as Dalzul looked at them.

"You know this," he said, and began softly to sing an old song, a song everybody from the barracks and camps of Terra knew, "Going to the Western Sea." Riel joined in, then Shan, then Forest in an unexpectedly deep, resonant voice. A few people near them turned to hear the harmonies strike through the gabble of speaking voices. The mezklete came hurrying over, abandoning its cart, its eyes large and bright. They ended the song, smiling, on a long soft chord.

"That is entrainment," Dalzul said. "All we need to get to Ganam is music. All there is, in the end, is music."

Smiling, Forest and then Riel raised their glasses.

"To music!" said Shan, feeling drunk and wildly happy.

"To the crew of the *Galba*," said Dalzul, and they drank.

The minimum crew-bonding period of isyeye was of course observed, and during it they had plenty of time to discuss the churten problem, both with Dalzul and among themselves. They watched the ship's tapes and reread Dalzul's records of his brief stay on Ganam till they had them memorized, and then argued about the wisdom of doing so. "We're simply accepting everything he saw and said as objective fact," Forest pointed out. "What sort of control can we provide?"

"His report and the ship's tapes agree completely," Shan said.

"Because, if his theory is correct, he and the instruments were entrained. The reality of the ship and the instruments may be perceivable to us only as perceived by the person, the intelligent being, in transilience. If the Cetians are sure of one thing about churten, it's that when intelligence is involved in the process they don't understand it any more. Send out a robot ship, no problem. Send out amoebas and crickets, no problem. Send out high-intelligence beings and all the bets are off. Your ship was part of your reality—your ten different realities. Its instruments obediently recorded the dissonances, or were affected by them to the point of malfunction and nonfunction. Only when you all worked together to construct a joint, coherent reality could the ship begin to respond to it and record it. Right?"

"Yes. But it's very difficult," Shan said, "to live without the notion that there is, somewhere, if one could just find it, a fact."

"Only fiction," said Forest, unrelenting. "Fact is one of our finest fictions."

"But music comes first," Shan said. "And dancing is people being music. I think what Dalzul sees is that we can . . . we can dance to Ganam."

"I like that," said Riel. "And look: on the fiction theory, we should be careful not to 'believe' Dalzul's records, or his ship's tapes. They're fictions. But, unless we accept the assumption, based only on the *Shoby* experiment, that the churten experience necessarily skews perception or judgment of perception, we have no reason to *dis*believe them. He's a seasoned observer and a superb gestalter."

"There are elements of a rather familiar kind of

fiction in his report," Forest said. "The princess who has apparently been waiting for him, expecting him, and leads him naked to her palace, where after due ceremonies and amenities she has sex with him—and very good sex too—? I'm not saying I disbelieve it. I don't. It looks and rings true. But it would be interesting to know how the princess perceived these events."

"We can't know that till we get there and talk to her," said Riel. "What are we waiting for, anyhow?"

The *Galba* was a Hainish in-system glass ship, newly fitted with churten controls. It was a pretty little bubble, not much bigger than the *Shoby*'s lander. Entering it, Shan had a few rather bad moments. The chaos, the senseless and centerless experience of churten, returned vividly to him: must he go through that again? Could he? Very sharp and aching was the thought of Tai, Tai who should be here now as she had been there then, Tai whom he had come to love aboard the *Shoby*, and Betton, the clear-hearted child— he needed them, they should be here.

Forest and Riel slipped through the hatch, and after them came Dalzul, the concentration of his energy almost visible around him as an aura or halo, a brightness of being. No wonder the Unists thought he was God, Shan thought, and thought also of the ceremonial, almost reverent welcome shown Dalzul by the Gaman. Dalzul was charged, full of mana, a power to which others responded, by which they were entrained. Shan's anxiety slipped from him. He knew that with Dalzul there would be no chaos.

"They thought we'd be able to control a bubble easier than the ship I had. I'll try not to bring her out right over the roofs this time. No wonder they thought I was a god, materializing in full view like that!" Shan had got used to the way Dalzul seemed to echo his thoughts, and Riel's and Forest's, and had come to expect it; they were in synchrony, it was their strength.

They took their places, Dalzul at the churten console, Riel plugged into the AI, Shan at the flight controls, and Forest as gestalt and Support. Dalzul looked round and nodded, and Shan took them out a few hundred kilometers from Ve Port. The curve of the planet fell away and the stars shone under his feet, around, above.

Dalzul began to sing, not a melody but a held note, a full, deep A. Riel joined in, an octave above, then Forest on the F between, and Shan found himself pouring out a steady middle C as if he were a church organ. Riel shifted to the C above, Dalzul and Forest sang the triad, and as the chord changed Shan did not know who sang which note, hearing and being only the sphere of the stars and the sweet frequencies swelling and fading in one long-held unison as Dalzul touched the console and the yellow sun was high in the blue sky above the city.

Shan had not stopped flying. Red and orange roofs, dusty plazas tilted under the ship. "How about over there, Shan," Dalzul said, pointing to a green strip by a canal, and Shan brought the *Galba* effortlessly down in a long glide and touched it onto grass, soft as a soap bubble.

He looked round at the others and out through the walls.

"Blue sky, green grass, near noon, natives approaching," said Dalzul. "Right?"

"Right," said Riel, and Shan laughed. No conflict of sensations, no chaos of perceptions, no terror of uncertainty, this time. "We churtened," he said. "We did it. We danced it!"

The field workers down by the canal got into a group and watched, evidently afraid to approach, but very soon people could be seen on the dusty road leading out from the city. "The welcoming committee, I trust," said Dalzul.

The four of them waited beside the bubble ship. The tension of the moment only heightened the extraordinary vividness of emotion and sensation. Shan felt that he knew the beautiful, harsh outlines of the two volcanoes that bounded the city's valley, knew them and would never forget them, knew the smell of the air and the fall of the light and the blackness of shadow under leaves; this is herenow, he said to himself with joyous certainty, I am herenow and there is no distance, no separation.

Tension without fear. Plumed and crested men, broad-chested and strong-armed, walked towards them steadily, their faces impassive, and stopped in front of them. One elderly man nodded his head slightly and said, "Sem Dazu." Dalzul made the gesture from heart to open embrace, saying, "Viaka!" The other men said, "Dazu, Sem Dazu," and some of them imitated Dalzul's gesture.

"Viaka," Dalzul said, "beya,"—friend—and he introduced his companions to them, repeating their names and the word friend.

"Foyes," said old Viaka. "Shan. Yeh." He knew he hadn't come very close to "Riel," and frowned slightly. "Friends. Be welcome. Come, come in Ganam." During his brief first stay, Dalzul had not been able to record much of the language for the Hainish linguists to work on; from his meager tapes they and their clever analoguers had produced a little manual of vocabulary and grammar, full of [?]s, which Shan had dutifully studied. He remembered beya, and kiyugi, be welcome [?], be at home [?]. Riel, a hilfer/linguist, would have liked longer to study the manual. "Better to learn the language from the speakers," Dalzul had said.

As they walked the dusty road to Ganam city the

vividness of impression began to overload on Shan, becoming a blur and glory of heat and radiance, red and yellow clay walls, pottery-red bare breasts and shoulders, purple and red and orange and umber striped and embroidered cloaks and vests and kilts, the gleam of gold and nod of feathers, the smells of oil and incense and dust and smoke and food and sweat, the sounds of many voices, slap of sandals and sluff of bare feet on stone and earth, bells, gongs, the difference of light, the touch and smell and beat of a world where nothing was known and everything was as it was, as it should be, this little city of stone and mud and splendid carvings, fiery in the light of its gold sun, crude, magnificent, and human. It was stranger than anything Shan had known and it was as if he had been away and come home again. Tears blurred his eyes. We are all one, he thought. There is no distance, no time between us; all we need do is step across, and we are here, together. He walked beside Dalzul and heard the people greet him, grave and quiet: Sem Dazu, they said, Sem Dazu, kiyugi. You have come home.

The first days were all overload. There were moments when Shan thought that he had stopped thinking—was merely experiencing, receiving, not processing. "Process later," Dalzul said with a laugh, when Shan told him. "How often does one get to be a child?" It was indeed like being a child, having no control over events and no responsibility for them. Expectable or incredible, they happened, and he was part of the happening and watched it happening at the same time. They were going to make Dalzul their king. It was ridiculous and it was perfectly natural. Your king dies without an heir; a silver man drops out of your sky and your princess says, "This is the man"; the silver man vanishes and returns with three strange companions who can work various miracles; you make him king. What else can you do with him?

Riel and Forest were, of course, reluctant, dubious about so deep an involvement with a native culture, but had no alternative to offer Dalzul. Since the kingship was evidently more honorary than authoritative, they admitted that he had probably better go along with what the Gaman wanted. Trying to keep some perspective on Dalzul's situation, they had separated themselves early on, living in a house near the market, where they could be with common people and enjoy a freedom of movement Dalzul did not have. The trouble with being king-to-be, he told Shan, was that he was expected to hang around the palace all day observing taboos.

Shan stayed with Dalzul. Viaka gave him one of the many wings of the rambling clay palace to himself. He shared it with a relative of Viaka's wife called Abud, who helped him keep house. Nothing was expected of him, either by Dalzul or by his native hosts; his time was free. The CRG had asked them to spend thirty days in Ganam. The days flowed by like shining water. He tried to keep his journal for the Ekumen, but found he hated to break the continuity of experience by talking about it, analyzing it. The whole point was that nothing happened, he thought, smiling.

The only experience that stood out as in some way different was a day he spent with old Viaka's niece [?] and her husband [?]—he had tried to get the kinship system straight, but the question marks remained, and for some reason this young couple seemed not to use their names. They took him on a long and beautiful walk to a waterfall up on the slope of the larger volcano, Iyananam. He understood that it was a sacred place they wanted him to see. He was very much surprised to find that the

sacred waterfall was employed to power a sacred
dynamo. The Gaman, as far as his companions
could explain and he could understand, had a quite
adequate grasp of the principles of hydroelectricity,
though they were woefully short of conductors, and
had no particular practical use for the power they
generated. Their discussion seemed to be about the
nature of electricity rather than the application of it,
but he could follow very little of it. He tried to ask if
there was any place they used electricity, but all he
could say was, "somewhere come out?" At such
moments he did not find it so agreeable to feel like a
child, or a half-wit. Yes, the young woman said, it
comes out at the ishkanem when the basemmiak
vada. Shan nodded and made notes. Like all Gaman,
his companions enjoyed watching him talk into his
noter and seeing the tiny symbols appear on the tiny
screen, an amiable magic.

They took him onto a terrace built out from the little dynamo building, which was built of dressed stone
laid in marvelously intricate courses. They tried to
explain something, pointing downstream. He saw
something shining in the quick glitter of the water,
but could not make out what it was. Heda, taboo, they
said, a word he knew well from Dalzul, though he had
not himself run into anything heda till now. As they
went on, he caught the name "Dazu" in their conversation with each other, but again could not follow.
They passed a little earth shrine, where in the infor-
mal worship of the Gaman each of them laid a leaf
from a nearby tree, and then set off down the moun-
tainside in the long light of late afternoon.

As they rounded a turn of the steep trail, he
could see in the hazy golden distance down the
great valley two other settlements, towns or cities.
He was surprised to see them, and then surprised by
his surprise. He realized that he had been so
absorbed in being in Ganam that he had forgotten it

was not the only place in the world. Pointing, he asked his companions, "Belong Gaman?" After some discussion, probably of what on earth he meant, they said no, only Ganam belonged to the Gaman; those cities were other cities.

Was Dalzul, then, right in thinking the world was called Ganam, or did that name mean just the city and its lands? "Tegud ao? What you call?" he asked, patting the ground, sweeping his arms around the circle of valley, the mountain at their backs, the other mountain facing them. "Nanam tegudyeh," said Viaka's niece [?], tentatively, but her husband [?] disagreed, and they discussed it impenetrably for a mile or more. Shan gave up, put away his noter, and enjoyed the walk in the cool of the evening down towards the golden walls of Ganam.

The next day, or maybe it was the day after, Dalzul came by while Shan was pruning the fruit tree in the walled courtyard of his bit of the palace. The pruning knife was a thin, slightly curved steel blade with a gracefully carved, well-worn wooden handle; it was sharp as a razor. "This is a lovely tool," he said to Dalzul. "My grandmother taught me to prune. It's not an art I've been able to practice much since I joined the Ekumen. They're good orcharders here. I was out talking with some of them yesterday." Had it been yesterday? Not that it mattered. Time is not duration but intensity; time is the beat and the interval, Shan had been thinking as he studied the tree, learning the inner rhythm of its growth, the patterned intervals of its branches. The years are flowers, the worlds are fruit . . . "Pruning makes me poetical," he said, and then, looking at Dalzul, said, "Is something wrong?" It was like a skipped pulse, a wrong note, a step mistaken in the dance.

"I don't know," Dalzul said. "Let's sit down a

minute." They went to the shade under the balcony and settled down cross-legged on the flagstones. "Probably," Dalzul said, "I've relied too far on my intuitive understanding of these people—followed my nose, instead of holding back, learning the language word by word, going by the book. . . . I don't know. But something is amiss."

Shan watched the strong, vivid face as Dalzul spoke. The fierce sunlight had tanned his white skin to a more human color. He wore his own shirt and trousers, but had let his grey hair fall loose as Gaman men did, wearing a narrow headband interwoven with gold, which gave him a regal and barbaric look.

"These are a barbaric people," he said. "More violent, more primitive perhaps, than I wanted to admit. This kingship they're determined to invest me with—I'm afraid I have to see it as something more than an honor or a sacral gesture. It is political, after all. At least, it would seem that by being chosen to be king, I've made a rival. An enemy."

"Who?"

"Aketa."

"I don't know him. He's not in the palace here?"

"No. He's not one of Viaka's people. He seems to have been away when I first came. As I understand Viaka, this man considers himself the heir to the throne and the legitimate mate of the princess."

"Princess Ket?" Shan had never yet spoken to the princess, who kept herself aloof, staying always in her part of the palace, though she allowed Dalzul to visit her there. "What does she say about this Aketa? Isn't she on your side? She chose you, after all."

"She says I am to be king. That hasn't changed. But she has. She's left the palace. In fact she's gone to live, as well as I can tell, in this Aketa's household! My God, Shan, is there any world in this universe where men can understand women?"

"Gethen," Shan said.

Dalzul laughed, but his face remained intense, pondering. "You have a partner," he said after a while. "Maybe that's the answer. I never came to a place with a woman where I knew, really knew, what she wanted, who she was. If you stick it out, do you finally get there?"

Shan was touched at the older man, the brilliant man, asking him such questions. "I don't know," he said. "Tai and I—we know each other in a way that— But it's not easy—I don't know. . . . But about the princess—Riel and Forest have been talking with people, learning the language. As women, maybe they'd have some insights?"

"Women yes and no," Dalzul said. "It's why I chose them, Shan. With two real women, the psychological dynamics might have been too complicated."

Shan said nothing, feeling again that something was missing or he was missing something, misunderstanding. He wondered if Dalzul knew that most of Shan's sexuality had been with men until he met Tai.

"Consider," Dalzul said, "for instance, if the princess thought she should be jealous of one or both of them, thought they were my sexual partners. That could be a snake's nest! As it is, they're no threat. Of course, seeking consonance, I'd have preferred all men. But the Elders on Hain are mostly old women, and I knew I had to suit them. So I asked you and your partner, a married couple. When your partner couldn't come, these two seemed the best solution. And they've performed admirably. But I don't think they're equipped to tell me what's going on in the mind, or the hormones, of a very fully sexed woman such as the princess."

The beat skipped again. Shan rubbed one hand against the rough stone of the terrace, puzzled at his own sense of confusion. Trying to return to the original subject, he asked, "If it is a political kingship, not a sacral one, can you possibly—just withdraw your candidacy, as it were?"

"Oh, it's sacred. The only way I could withdraw is to run away. Churten back to Ve Port."

"We could fly the *Galba* to another part of the planet," Shan suggested. "Observe somewhere else."

"From what Viaka tells me, leaving's not really an option. Ket's defection has apparently caused a schism, and if Aketa gains power, his supporters will wreak vengeance on Viaka and all his people. Blood sacrifice for offense to the true and sacred king's person. . . . Religion and politics! How could I of all men be so blind? I let my longings persuade me that we'd found a rather primitive idyll. But what we're in the middle of here is a factional and sexual competition among intelligent barbarians who keep their pruning hooks and their swords extremely sharp." Dalzul smiled suddenly, and his light eyes flashed. "They are wonderful, these people. They are everything we lost with our literacy, our industry, our science. Directly sensual—utterly passionate— primally real. I love them. If they want to make me their king, then by God I'll put a basket of feathers on my head and be their king! But before that, I've got to figure out how to handle Aketa and his crew. And the only key to Aketa seems to be our moody Princess Ket. Whatever you can find out, tell me, Shan. I need your advice and your help."

"You have it, sir," Shan said, touched again. After Dalzul had left, he decided that what he should do was what Dalzul's unexpected male-heterosexual defensiveness prevented him from doing: go ask advice and help of Forest and Riel.

He set off for their house. As he made his way through the marvelously noisy and aromatic market, he asked himself when he had seen them last, and realized it had been several days. What had he been doing? He had been in the orchards. He had been up on the mountain, on Iyananam, where there was a dynamo . . . where he had seen other cities. . . . The pruning hook was steel. How did the Gaman make their steel? Did they have a foundry? Did they get it in trade? His mind was sluggishly, laboriously turning over these matters as he came into the courtyard, where Forest sat on a cushion on the terrace, reading a book.

"Well," she said. "A visitor from another planet!"

It had been quite a long time since he had been here—eight, ten days?

"Where've you been?" he asked, confused.

"Right here. Riel!" Forest called up to the balcony. Several heads looked over the carved railing, and the one with curly hair said, "Shan! I'll be right down!"

Riel arrived with a pot of tipu seeds, the ubiquitous munchy of Ganam. The three of them sat around on the terrace, half in the sun and half out of it, and cracked seeds; typical anthropoids, Riel remarked. She greeted Shan with real warmth, and yet she and Forest were unmistakably cautious: they watched him, they asked nothing, they waited to see . . . what? How long had it been, then, since he had seen them? He felt a sudden tremor of unease, a missed beat so profound that he put his hands flat on the warm sandstone, bracing himself. Was it an earthquake? Built between two sleepy volcanoes, the city shuddered a little now and then, bits of clay fell off the walls, little orange tiles off the roofs. . . . Forest and Riel watched him. Nothing was shaking, nothing was falling.

"Dalzul has run into some kind of problem in the palace," he said.

"Has he," said Forest in a perfectly neutral tone.

"A native claimant to the throne, a pretender or heir, has turned up. And the princess is staying with him, now. But she still tells Dalzul that he's to be king. If this pretender gets power, apparently he threatens reprisals against all Viaka's people, anybody who backed Dalzul. It's just the kind of sticky situation Dalzul was hoping to avoid."

"And is matchless at resolving," said Forest.

"I think he feels pretty much at an impasse. He doesn't understand what role the princess is playing. I think that troubles him most. I thought you might have some idea why, after more or less hurling herself into his arms, she's gone off to stay with his rival."

"It's Ket you're talking about," Riel said, cautious.

"Yes. He calls her the princess. That's not what she is?"

"I don't know what Dalzul means by the word. It has a lot of connotations. If the denotation is 'a king's daughter,' then it doesn't fit. There is no king."

"Not at present—"

"Not ever," Forest said.

Shan suppressed a flash of anger. He was getting tired of being the half-wit child, and Forest could be abrasively gnomic. "Look," he said, "I—I've been sort of out of it. Bear with me. I thought their king was dead. And given Dalzul's apparently miraculous descent from heaven during the search for a new king, they saw him as divinely appointed, 'the one who will hold the scepter.' Is that all wrong?"

"Divinely appointed seems to be right," Riel said. "These are certainly sacred matters." She hesitated and looked at Forest. They worked as a team, Shan thought, but not, at the moment, a team that included him. What had become of the wonderful oneness?

"Who is this rival, this claimant?" Forest asked him.

"A man named Aketa."

"Aketa!"

"You know him?"

Again the glance between the two; then Forest turned to face him and looked directly into his eyes. "Shan," she said, "we are seriously out of sync. I wonder if we're having the churten problem. The chaos experience you had on the *Shoby*."

"Here, now? When we've been here for days, weeks—"

"Where's here?" Forest asked, serious and intent.

Shan slapped his hand on the flagstone. "Here! Now! In this courtyard of your house in Ganam! This is nothing like the chaos experience. We're sharing this— it's coherent, it's consonant, we're here together! Eating tipu seeds!"

"I think so too," Forest said, so gently that Shan realized she was trying to calm him, reassure him. "But we may be . . . reading the experience quite differently."

"People always do, everywhere," he said rather desperately.

She had moved so that he could see more clearly the book she had been reading when he came. It was an ordinary bound book, but they had brought no books with them on the *Galba*, a thick book on some kind of heavy brownish paper, hand-lettered, a Terran antique book from New Cairo Library, it was not a book but a pillow, a brick, a basket, not a book, it was a book. In a strange writing. In a strange language. A book with covers of carved wood, hinged with gold.

"What is that?" he asked almost inaudibly.

"The sacred history of the Cities Under Iyananam, we think," Forest said.

"A book," Riel said.

"They're illiterate," Shan said.

"Some of them are," said Forest.

"Quite a lot of them are, actually," said Riel.

"But some of the merchants and the priests can read. Aketa gave us this. We've been studying with him. He's a marvelous teacher."

"He's a kind of scholar priest, we think," said Forest. "There are these positions, we're calling them priesthoods because they're basically sacred, but they're really more like jobs, or vocations, callings. Very important to the Gaman, to the whole structure of society, we think. They have to be filled; things go out of whack if they aren't. And if you have the vocation, the talent, you go out of whack if you don't do it, too. A lot of them are kind of occasional, like a person that officiates at an annual festival, but some of them seem to be really demanding, and very prestigious. Most of them are for men. Our feeling is that probably the way a man gets prestige is to fill one of the priesthoods."

"But men run the whole city," Shan protested.

"I don't know," Forest said, still with the uncharacteristic gentleness that told Shan he was not in full control. "We'd describe it as a non-gender-dominant society. Not much division of labor on sexual lines. All kinds of marriages—polyandry may be the most common, two or three husbands. A good many women are out of heterosexual circulation because they have homosexual group marriages, the iyeha, three or four or more women. We haven't found a male equivalent yet—"

"Anyhow," said Riel, "Aketa is one of Ket's husbands. His name means something like Ket's-kin-first-husband. Kin, meaning they're in the same volcano lineage. He was down the valley in Sponta when we first arrived."

"And he's a priest, a high one, we think. Maybe because he's Ket's husband, and she's certainly an important one. But most of the really prestigious priesthoods seem to be for men. Probably to compensate for lack of childbearing."

The anger rose up again in Shan. Who were these women to lecture him on gender and womb envy? Like a sea wave the hatred filled him with salt bitterness, and sank away, and was gone. He sat with his fragile sisters in the sunlight on the stone, and looked at the heavy, impossible book open on Forest's lap.

After a long time he said, "What does it say?"

"I only know a word here and there. Aketa wanted me to have it for a while. He's been teaching us. Mostly I look at the pictures. Like a baby." She showed him the small, brightly painted, gilded picture on the open page: men in wonderful robes and headdresses, dancing, under the purple slopes of Iyananam.

"Dalzul thought they were preliterate," he said. "He has to see this."

"He has seen it," Riel said.

"But—" Shan began, and was silent.

"Long long ago on Terra," Riel said, "one of the first anthropologists took a man from a tiny, remote, isolated Arctic tribe to a huge city, New York City. The thing that most impressed this very intelligent tribesman about New York City were the knobs on the bottom posts of staircases. He studied them with deep interest. He wasn't interested in the vast buildings, the streets full of crowds, the machines. . . ."

"We wonder if the churten problem centers not on impressions only, but expectations," Forest said. "We make sense of the world intentionally. Faced with chaos, we seek or make the familiar, and build up the world with it. Babies do it, we all do it; we filter out most of what our senses report. We're conscious only of what we need to be or want to be conscious of. In churten, the universe dissolves. As we come out, we reconstruct it—frantically. Grabbing at things we recognize. And once one part of it is there, the rest gets built on that."

"I say 'I,'" said Riel, "and an infinite number of sentences could follow. But the next word begins to build the immutable syntax. 'I want—' By the last word of the sentence, there may be no choice at all. And also, you can only use words you know."

"That's how we came out of the chaos experience on the *Shoby*," Shan said. His head had begun suddenly to ache, a painful, irregular throb at the temples. "We talked. We constructed the syntax of the experience. We told our story."

"And tried very hard to tell it truly," Forest said.

After a pause, pressing the pressure points on his temples, Shan said, "You're saying that Dalzul has been lying?"

"No. But is he telling the Ganam story or the Dalzul story? The childlike, simple people acclaiming him king, the beautiful princess offering herself . . . "

"But she did—"

"It's her job. Her vocation. She's one of these priests, an important one. Her title is Anam. Dalzul translated it princess. We think it means earth. The earth, the ground, the world. She is Ganam's earth, receiving the stranger in honor. But there's more to it—this reciprocal function, which Dalzul interprets as kingship. They simply don't have kings. It must be some kind of priesthood role as Anam's mate. Not Ket's husband, but her mate when she's Anam. But we don't know. We don't know what responsibility he's taken on."

"And we may be inventing just as much of it as Dalzul is," Riel said. "How can we be sure?"

"If we have you back to compare notes with, it'll be a big relief," said Forest. "We need you."

So does he, Shan thought. He needs my help, they need my help. What help have I to give? I don't know where I am. I know nothing about this place. I know the stone is warm and rough under the palm of my hand.

I know these two women are sympathetic, intelligent, trying to be honest.

I know Dalzul is a great man, not a foolish egoist, not a liar.

I know the stone is rough, the sun is warm, the shadow cool. I know the slight, sweet taste of tipu seeds, the crunch between the teeth.

I know that when he was thirty, Dalzul was worshiped as God. No matter how he disavowed that worship, it must have changed him. Growing old, he would remember what it was to be a king. . . .

"Do we know anything at all about this priesthood he's supposed to fill, then?" he asked harshly.

"The key word seems to be 'todok,' stick or staff or scepter. Todoghay, the one who holds the scepter, is the title. Dalzul got that right. It does sound like a king. But we don't think it means ruling people."

"Day-to-day decisions are made by the councils," Riel said. "The priests educate and lead ceremony and—keep the city in spiritual balance?"

"Sometimes, possibly, by blood sacrifice," Forest said. "We don't know what they've asked him to do! But it does seem he'd better find out."

After a while Shan sighed. "I feel like a fool," he said.

"Because you fell in love with Dalzul?" Forest's black eyes gazed straight into his. "I honor you for it. But I think he needs your help."

When he left, walking slowly, he felt Forest and Riel watch him go, felt their affectionate concern following him, staying with him.

He headed back for the big market square. We must tell our story together, he told himself. But the words were hollow.

I must listen, he thought. Not talk, not tell. Be still.

He listened as he walked in the streets of Ganam. He tried to look, to see with his eyes, to feel, to be in his own skin in this world, in this world, itself. Not his world, not Dalzul's, or Forest's or Riel's, but this world as it was in its recalcitrant and irreducible earth and stone and clay, its dry bright air, its breathing bodies and thinking minds. A vendor was calling wares in a brief musical phrase, five beats, tataBANaba, and an equal pause, and the call again, sweet and endless. A woman passed him and Shan saw her, saw her absolutely for a moment: short, with muscular arms and hands, a preoccupied look on her wide face with its thousand tiny wrinkles etched by the sun on the pottery smoothness of the skin. She strode past him, purposeful, not noticing him, and was gone. She left behind her an indubitable sense of being. Of being herself. Unconstructed, unreadable, unreachable. The other. Not his to understand.

All right then. Rough stone warm against the palm, and a five-beat measure, and a short old woman going about her business. It was a beginning.

I've been dreaming, he thought. Ever since we got here. Not a nightmare like the *Shoby*. A good dream, a sweet dream. But was it my dream or his? Following him around, seeing through his eyes, meeting Viaka and the others, being feasted, listening to the music . . . Learning their dances, learning to drum with them . . . Learning to cook . . . Pruning orchards . . . Sitting on my terrace, eating tipu seeds . . . A sunny dream, full of music and trees and simple companionship and peaceful solitude. My good dream, he thought, surprised and wry. No kingship, no beautiful princess, no rivals for the throne. I'm a lazy man. With lazy dreams. I need Tai to wake me up, make me vibrate, irritate me. I need my angry woman, my unforgiving friend.

Forest and Riel weren't a bad substitute. They were certainly friends, and though they forgave his laziness, they had jolted him out of it.

An odd question appeared in his mind: Does

Dalzul know we're here? Apparently Forest and Riel don't exist for him as women; do I exist for him as a man?

He did not try to answer the question. My job, he thought, is to try to jolt him. To put a bit of dissonance in the harmony, to syncopate the beat. I'll ask him to dinner and talk to him, he thought.

Middle-aged, majestic, hawk-nosed, fierce-faced, Aketa was the most mild and patient of teachers. "Todokyu nkenes ebegebyu," he repeated for the fifth or sixth time, smiling.

"The scepter—something—is full of? has mastery over? represents?" said Forest.

"Is connected with—symbolizes?" said Riel.

"Kenes!" Shan said. "Electric! That's the word they kept using at the generator. Power!"

"The scepter symbolizes power?" said Forest. "Well, what a revelation. Shit!"

"Shit," Aketa repeated, evidently liking the sound of the word. "Shit!"

Shan went into mime, dancing a waterfall, imitating the motion of wheels, the hum and buzz of the little dynamo up on the volcano. The two women stared at him as he roared, turned, hummed, buzzed, and crackled, shouting "Kenes?" at intervals like a demented chicken. But Aketa's smile broadened. "Soha, kenes," he agreed, and mimicked the leap of a spark from one fingertip to another. "Todokyu nkenes ebegebyu."

"The scepter signifies, symbolizes electricity! It must mean something like—if you take up the scepter you're the Electricity Priest—like Aketa's the Library Priest and Agot's the Calendar Priest—right?"

"It would make sense," Forest said.

"Why would they pick Dalzul straight off as their chief electrician?" Riel asked.

"Because he came out of the sky, like lightning!"
said Shan.

"Did they pick him?" Forest asked.

There was a pause. Aketa looked from one to the
other, alert and patient.

"What's 'choose'?" Forest asked Riel, who said,
"Sotot."

Forest turned to their teacher. "Aketa: Dazu . . .
ntodok . . . sotot?"

Aketa was silent for some time and then said,
gravely and clearly, "Soha. Todok nDazu oyo sotot."

"'Yes. And also the scepter chooses Dalzul,'" Riel
murmured.

"Aheo?" Shan demanded—why? But of Aketa's
answer they could understand only a few words:
priesthood or vocation, sacredness, the earth.

"Anam," Riel said—"Ket? Anam Ket?"

Aketa's pitch-black eyes met hers. Again he was
silent, and the quality of his silence held them all
still. When he spoke it was with sorrow. "Ai Dazu!"
he said. "Ai Dazu kesemmas!"

He stood up, and knowing what was expected,
they too rose, thanked him quietly for his teaching,
and filed out. Obedient children, Shan thought.
Good pupils. Learning what knowledge?

That evening he looked up from his practice on the
little Gaman finger-drum, to which Abud liked to listen, sitting with him on the terrace, sometimes
singing a soft chant when he caught a familiar beat.

"Abud," he said, "metu?"—a word?

Abud, who had got used to the inquiry in the last
few days, said, "Soha." He was a humorless, even-
natured young man; he tolerated all Shan's peculiari-
ties, perhaps, Shan thought, because he really hardly
noticed them.

"'Kesemmas,'" Shan said.

"Ah," said Abud, and repeated the word, and then went off slowly and relentlessly into the incomprehensible. Shan had learned to watch him rather than trying to catch the words. He listened to the tone, saw the gestures, the expressions. The earth, down, low, digging? The Gaman buried their dead. Dead, death? He mimed dying, a corpse; but Abud never understood his charades, and stared blankly. Shan gave up, and pattered out the dance rhythm of yesterday's festival on the drum. "Soha, soha," said Abud.

"I've never actually spoken to Ket," Shan said to Dalzul.

It had been a good dinner. He had cooked it, with considerable assistance from Abud, who had prevented him just in time from frying the fezuni. Eaten raw, dipped in fiery pepperjuice, the fezuni had been delicious. Abud had eaten with them, respectfully silent as he always was in Dalzul's presence, and then excused himself. Shan and Dalzul were now nibbling tipu seeds and drinking nut beer, sitting on little carpets on the terrace in the purple twilight, watching the stars slowly clot the sky with brilliance.

"All men except the chosen king are taboo to her," Dalzul said.

"But she's married," Shan said—"isn't she?"

"No, no. The princess must remain virgin until the king is chosen. Then she belongs only to him. The sacred marriage, the hierogamy."

"They do practice polyandry," Shan said uncertainly.

"Her union with him is probably the fundamental event of the kingship ceremonial. Neither has any real choice in the matter. That's why her defection is so troubling. She's breaking her own society's rules." Dalzul took a long draft of beer. "What

made me their choice in the first place—my dramatic
appearance out of the sky—may be working against
me now. I broke the rules by going away, and then
coming back, and not coming back alone. One
supernatural person pops out of the sky, all right,
but four of them, male and female, all eating and
drinking and shitting like everybody else, and asking stupid questions in baby talk all the time? We
aren't behaving in a properly sacred manner. And
they respond by impropriety of the same order, rule-
breaking. Primitive worldviews are rigid, they break
when strained. We're having a disintegrative effect
on this society. And I am responsible."

Shan took a breath. "It isn't your world, sir," he
said. "It's theirs. They're responsible for it." He
cleared his throat. "And they don't seem all that
primitive—they make steel, their grasp of the principles of electricity is impressive—and they are liter-
ate, and the social system seems to be very flexible
and stable, if what Forest and—"

"I still call her the princess, but as I learn the
language better I've realized that that's inaccurate,"
Dalzul said, setting down his cup and speaking mus-
ingly. "Queen is probably nearer: queen of Ganam,
of the Gaman. She is identified as Ganam, as the soil
of the planet itself."

"Yes," Shan said. "Riel says—"

"So that in a sense she is the Earth. As, in a sense,
I am Space, the sky. Coming alone to this world, a
conjunction. A mystic union: fire and air with soil
and water. The old mythologies enacted yet again in
living flesh. She cannot turn away from me. It dislo-
cates the very order of things. The father and the
mother are joined, their children are obedient,
happy, secure. But if the mother rebels, disorder, distress, failure ensue. These responsibilities are absolute. We don't choose them. They choose us. She must
be brought back to her duty to her people."

"As Forest and Riel understand it, she's been married to Aketa for several years, and her second husband is the father of her daughter." Shan heard the harshness of his voice; his mouth was dry and his heart pounding as if he was afraid, of what? of being disobedient?

"Viaka says he can bring her back to the palace," Dalzul said, "but at risk of retaliation from the pretender's faction."

"Dalzul!" Shan said. "Ket is a married woman! She went back to her family. Her duty to you as Earth Priestess or whatever it is is done. Aketa is her husband, not your rival. He doesn't want the scepter, the crown, whatever it is!"

Dalzul made no reply and his expression was unreadable in the deepening twilight.

Shan went on, desperately: "Until we understand this society better, maybe you should hold back—certainly not let Viaka kidnap Ket—"

"I'm glad you see that," Dalzul said. "Although I can't help my involvement, we certainly must try not to interfere with these people's belief systems. Power is responsibility, alas! Well, I should be off. Thank you for a very pleasant evening, Shan. We can still sing a tune together, eh, shipmates?" He stood up and patted the air on the back, saying, "Good night, Forest; good night, Riel," before he patted Shan on the back and said, "Good night and thanks, Shan!" He strode out of the courtyard, a lithe, erect figure, a white glimmer in the starlit dark.

"I think we've got to get him onto the ship, Forest. He's increasingly delusional." Shan squeezed his hands together till the knuckles cracked. "I think he's delusional. Maybe I am. But you and Riel and I, we seem to be in the same general reality—fiction—are we?"

Forest nodded grimly. "Increasingly so," she said. "And if kesemmas does mean dying, or murder—Riel thinks it's murder, it involves violence. . . . I have this horrible vision of poor Dalzul committing some awful ritual sacrifice, cutting somebody's throat while convinced that he's pouring out oil or cutting cloth or something harmless. I'd be glad to get him out of this! I'd be glad to get out myself. But how?"

"Surely if the three of us—"

"Reason with him?" Forest asked, sardonic.

When they went to what he called the palace, they had to wait a long time to see Dalzul. Old Viaka, anxious and nervous, tried to send them away, but they waited. Dalzul came out into his courtyard at last and greeted Shan. He did not acknowledge or did not perceive Riel and Forest. If he was acting, it was a consummate performance; he moved without awareness of their physical presence and talked through their speech. When at last Shan said, "Forest and Riel are here, Dalzul—here—look at them!"— Dalzul looked where he gestured and then looked back at Shan with such shocked compassion that Shan lost his own bearings and turned to see if the women were still there.

Dalzul, watching him, spoke very gently: "It's about time we went back, Shan."

"Yes—Yes, I think so—I think we ought to." Tears of pity, relief, shame jammed in Shan's throat for a moment. "We should go back. It isn't working."

"Very soon," Dalzul said, "very soon now. Don't worry, Shan. Anxiety increases the perceptual anomalies. Just take it easy, as you did at first, and remember that you've done nothing wrong. As soon as the coronation has—"

"No! We should go now—"

"Shan, whether I asked for it or not, I have an obligation here, and I will fulfill it. If I run out on them, Aketa's faction will have their swords out—"

"Aketa doesn't have a sword," Riel said, her voice high and loud as Shan had never heard it. "These people don't have swords, they don't make them!"

Dalzul talked on through her voice: "As soon as the ceremony is over and the kingship is filled, we'll go. After all, I can go and be back within an hour, if need be. I'll take you back to Ve Port. In no time at all, as the joke is. So stop worrying about what never was your problem. I got you into this. It's my responsibility."

"How can—" Shan began, but Forest's long, black hand was on his arm.

"Don't try, Shan," she said. "The mad reason much better than the sane. Come on. This is very hard to take."

Dalzul was turning serenely away, as if they had left him already.

"Either we have to wait for this ceremony with him," Forest said as they went out into the hot, bright street, "or we knock him on the head and stick him in the ship."

"I'd *like* to knock him on the head," Riel said.

"If we do get him onto the ship," Shan said, "how do we know he'll take us back to Ve? And if he turns round and comes right back, how do we know what he'll do? He could destroy Ganam instead of saving it—"

"Shan!" Riel said, "Stop it! Is Ganam a world? Is Dalzul a god?"

He stared at her. A couple of women going by looked at them, and one nodded a greeting, "Ha, Foyes! Ha, Yeh!"

"Ha, Tasasap!" Forest said to her, while Riel, her eyes blazing, faced Shan: "Ganam is one little city-

state on a large planet, which the Gaman call Anam,
and the people in the next valley call something else
entirely. We've seen one tiny corner of it. It'll take us
years to know anything about it. Dalzul, because
he's crazy or because churtening made him crazy or
made us all crazy, I don't know which, I don't care
just now—Dalzul barged in and got mixed up in
sacred stuff and maybe is causing some trouble and
confusion. But these people *live* here. This is their
place. One man can't destroy them and one man
can't save them! They have their own story, and
they're telling it! How we'll figure in it I don't know—
maybe as some idiots that fell out of the sky once!"

Forest put a peaceable arm around Riel's shoulders. "When she gets excited she gets excited. Come
on, Shan. Aketa certainly isn't planning to slaughter
Viaka's household. I don't see these people letting us
mess up anything in a big way. They're in control.
We'll go through this ceremony. It probably isn't a big
deal, except in Dalzul's mind. And as soon as it's over
and his mind's at rest, ask him to take us home. He'll
do it. He's—" She paused. "He's fatherly," she said,
without sarcasm.

They did not see Dalzul again until the day of the
ceremony. He stayed holed up in his palace, and
Viaka sternly forbade them entrance. Aketa evidently
had no power to interfere in another sacred jurisdic-
tion, and no wish to. "Tezyeme," he said, which
meant something on the order of "it is happening
the way it is supposed to happen." He did not look
happy about it, but he was not going to interfere.

On the morning of the Ceremony of the
Scepter, there was no buying and selling in the
marketplace. People came out in their finest kilts
and gorgeous vests; all the men of the priesthoods
wore the high, plumed, basketry headdresses and

massive gold earrings. Babies' and children's heads
were rubbed with red ocher. But it was not a festiv-
ity, such as the Star-Rising ceremony of a few days
earlier; nobody danced, nobody cooked tipu-bread,
there was no music. Only a large, rather subdued
crowd kept gathering in the marketplace. At last
the doors of Aketa's house—Ket's house, actually,
Riel reminded them—swung open, and a procession came forth, walking to the complex, thrilling,
somber beat of drums. The drummers had been
waiting in the streets behind the house, and came
forward to walk behind the procession. The whole
city seemed to shake to the steady, heavy rhythms.

Shan had never seen Ket except on the ship's
tape of Dalzul's first arrival, but he recognized her at
once in the procession: a stern, splendid woman. She
wore a headdress less elaborate than most of the
men's, but ornate with gold, balancing it proudly as
she walked. Beside her walked Aketa, red plumes
nodding above his wicker crown, and another man to
her left—"Ketketa, second husband," Riel murmured.
"That's their daughter." The child was four or five,
very dignified, pacing along with her parents, her
dark hair rough and red with ocher. "All the priests
in Ket's volcano lineage are here," Riel went on.
"There's the Earth-Turner. That old one, that's the
Calendar Priest. There's a lot of them I don't know.
This is a *big* ceremony. . . ." Her whisper was a little
shaky.

The procession turned left out of the marketplace and moved on to the heavy beating of the
drums until Ket came abreast of the main entrance
of Viaka's rambling, yellow-walled house. There,
with no visible signal, everyone stopped walking at
once. The drums maintained the heavy, complex
beat; but one by one they dropped out, till one
throbbed alone like a heart and then stopped, leaving a terrifying silence.

A man with a towering headdress of woven feathers stepped forward and called out a summons: "Sem ayatan! Sem Dazu!"

The door opened slowly. Dalzul stood framed in the sunlit doorway, darkness behind him. He wore his black-and-silver uniform. His hair shone silver.

In the absolute silence of the crowd, Ket walked forward to face him. She knelt down on both knees, bowed her head, and said, "Dazu, sototiyu!"

" 'Dalzul, you chose,' " Riel whispered.

Dalzul smiled. He stepped forward and reached out his hands to lift Ket to her feet.

A whisper ran like wind in the crowd, a hiss or gasp or sigh of shock. Ket's gold-burdened head came up, startled, then she was on her feet, fiercely erect, her hands at her sides. "Sototiyu!" she said, and turned, and strode back to her husbands.

The drums took up a soft patter, a rain sound.

A gap opened in the procession just in front of the door of the house. Quiet and self-possessed, walking with great dignity, Dalzul came forward and took the place left open for him. The rain sound of the drums grew louder, turning to thunder, thunder rolling near and far, loud and low. With the perfect unanimity of a school of fish or flock of birds the procession moved forward.

The people of the city followed, Shan, Riel, and Forest among them.

"Where are they going?" Forest said as they left the last street and struck out on the narrow road between the orchards.

"This road goes up Iyananam," Shan said.

"Onto the volcano? Maybe that's where the ritual will be."

The drums beat, the sunlight beat, Shan's heart beat, his feet struck the dust of the road, all in one huge pulse. Entrained. Thought and speech lost in the one great beat, beat, beat.

The procession had halted. The followers were stopping. The three Terrans kept on until they came up alongside the procession itself. It was re-forming, the drummers drawing off to one side, a few of them softly playing the thunder roll. Some of the crowd, people with children, were beginning to go back down the steep trail beside the mountain stream. Nobody spoke, and the noise of the waterfall uphill from them and the noisy torrent nearby almost drowned out the drums.

They were a hundred paces or so downhill from the little stone building that housed the dynamo. The plumed priests, Ket and her husbands and household, all had drawn aside, leaving the way clear to the bank of the stream. Stone steps were built down right to the water, and at their foot lay a terrace, paved with light-colored stone, over which the clear water washed in quick-moving, shallow sheets. Amidst the shine and motion of the water stood an altar or low pedestal, blinding bright in the noon sun: gilt or solid gold, carved and drawn into intricate and fantastic figures of crowned men, dancing men, men with diamond eyes. On the pedestal lay a wand, not gold, unornamented, of dark wood or tarnished metal.

Dalzul began to walk towards the pedestal.

Aketa stepped forward suddenly and stood at the head of the stone steps, blocking Dalzul's way. He spoke in a ringing voice, a few words. Riel shook her head, not understanding. Dalzul stood silent, motionless, and made no reply. When Aketa fell silent, Dalzul strode straight forward, as if to walk through him.

Aketa held his ground. He pointed to Dalzul's feet. "Tediad!" he said sharply—" 'Shoes,'" Riel murmured. Aketa and all the Gaman in the procession were barefoot. After a moment, with no loss of dignity, Dalzul knelt, took off his shoes and stockings, set them aside, and stood up, barefoot in his black uniform.

"Stand aside now," he said quietly, and, as if understanding him, Aketa stepped back among the watchers.

"Ai Dazu," he said as Dalzul passed him, and Ket said softly, "Ai Dazu!" The soft murmur followed Dalzul as he paced down the steps and out onto the terrace, walking through the shallow water that broke in bright drops around his ankles. Unhesitating, he walked to the pedestal and around it, so that he faced the procession and the watching people. He smiled, and put out his hand, and seized the scepter.

"No," Shan said. "No, we had no spy-eye with us. Yes, he died instantly. No, I have no idea what voltage. Underground wires from the generator, we assume. Yes, of course it was deliberate, intentional, arranged. They thought he had chosen that death. He chose it when he chose to have sex with Ket, with the Earth Priestess, with the Earth. They thought he knew; how could they know he didn't know? If you lie with the Earth, you die by the Lightning. Men come from a long way to Ganam for that death. Dalzul came from a very long way. No, we none of us understood. No, I don't know if it had anything to do with the churten effect, with perceptual dissonance, with chaos. We came to see things differently; but which of us knew the truth? He knew he had to be a god again."

ANOTHER STORY OR
A FISHERMAN OF THE
INLAND SEA

*To the Stabiles of the Ekumen on Hain, and to Gvonesh,
Director of the Churten Field Laboratories at Ve Port:
from Tiokunan'n Hideo, Farmholder of the Second
Sedoretu of Udan, Derdan'nad, Oket, on O.*

I shall make my report as if I told a story, this having
been the tradition for some time now. You may,
however, wonder why a farmer on the planet O is
reporting to you as if he were a Mobile of the Ekumen. My story will explain that. But it does not
explain itself. Story is our only boat for sailing on
the river of time, but in the great rapids and the
winding shallows, no boat is safe.

So: once upon a time when I was twenty-one
years old I left my home and came on the NAFAL
ship *Terraces of Darranda* to study at the Ekumenical
Schools on Hain.

The distance between Hain and my home world
is just over four light-years, and there has been traf-
fic between O and the Hainish system for twenty

centuries. Even before the Nearly As Fast As Light drive, when ships spent a hundred years of planetary time instead of four to make the crossing, there were people who would give up their old life to come to a new world. Sometimes they returned; not often. There were tales of such sad returns to a world that had forgotten the voyager. I knew also from my mother a very old story called "The Fisherman of the Inland Sea," which came from her home world, Terra. The life of a ki'O child is full of stories, but of all I heard told by her and my othermother and my fathers and grandparents and uncles and aunts and teachers, that one was my favorite. Perhaps I liked it so well because my mother told it with deep feeling, though very plainly, and always in the same words (and I would not let her change the words if she ever tried to).

The story tells of a poor fisherman, Urashima, who went out daily in his boat alone on the quiet sea that lay between his home island and the mainland. He was a beautiful young man with long, black hair, and the daughter of the king of the sea saw him as he leaned over the side of the boat and she gazed up to see the floating shadow cross the wide circle of the sky.

Rising from the waves, she begged him to come to her palace under the sea with her. At first he refused, saying, "My children wait for me at home." But how could he resist the sea king's daughter? "One night," he said. She drew him down with her under the water, and they spent a night of love in her green palace, served by strange undersea beings. Urashima came to love her dearly, and maybe he stayed more than one night only. But at last he said, "My dear, I must go. My children wait for me at home."

"If you go, you go forever," she said.

"I will come back," he promised.

She shook her head. She grieved, but did not plead with him. "Take this with you," she said, giving him a little box, wonderfully carved, and sealed shut. "Do not open it, Urashima."

So he went up onto the land, and ran up the shore to his village, to his house: but the garden was a wilderness, the windows were blank, the roof had fallen in. People came and went among the familiar houses of the village, but he did not know a single face. "Where are my children?" he cried. An old woman stopped and spoke to him: "What is your trouble, young stranger?"

"I am Urashima, of this village, but I see no one here I know!"

"Urashima!" the woman said—and my mother would look far away, and her voice as she said the name made me shiver, tears starting to my eyes— "Urashima! My grandfather told me a fisherman named Urashima was lost at sea, in the time of his grandfather's grandfather. There has been no one of that family alive for a hundred years."

So Urashima went back down to the shore; and there he opened the box, the gift of the sea king's daughter. A little white smoke came out of it and drifted away on the sea wind. In that moment Urashima's black hair turned white, and he grew old, old, old; and he lay down on the sand and died.

Once, I remember, a traveling teacher asked my mother about the fable, as he called it. She smiled and said, "In the Annals of the Emperors of my nation of Terra it is recorded that a young man named Urashima, of the Yosa district, went away in the year 477, and came back to his village in the year 825, but soon departed again. And I have heard that the box was kept in a shrine for many centuries." Then they talked about something else.

My mother, Isako, would not tell the story as often as I demanded it. "That one is so sad," she would say,

and tell instead about Grandmother and the rice
dumpling that rolled away, or the painted cat who
came alive and killed the demon rats, or the peach
boy who floated down the river. My sister and my germanes, and older people, too, listened to her tales as
closely as I did. They were new stories on O, and a
new story is always a treasure. The painted cat story
was the general favorite, especially when my mother
would take out her brush and the block of strange,
black, dry ink from Terra, and sketch the animals—
cat, rat—that none of us had ever seen: the wonderful
cat with arched back and brave round eyes, the
fanged and skulking rats, "pointed at both ends" as
my sister said. But I waited always, through all other
stories, for her to catch my eye, look away, smile a little and sigh, and begin, "Long, long ago, on the shore
of the Inland Sea there lived a fisherman . . ."

Did I know then what that story meant to her?
that it was her story? that if she were to return to her
village, her world, all the people she had known
would have been dead for centuries?

Certainly I knew that she "came from another
world," but what that meant to me as a five-, or
seven-, or ten-year-old, is hard for me now to imagine, impossible to remember. I knew that she was a
Terran and had lived on Hain; that was something
to be proud of. I knew that she had come to O as a
Mobile of the Ekumen (more pride, vague and
grandiose) and that "your father and I fell in love at
the Festival of Plays in Sudiran." I knew also that
arranging the marriage had been a tricky business.
Getting permission to resign her duties had not
been difficult—the Ekumen is used to Mobiles going
native. But as a foreigner, Isako did not belong to a
ki'O moiety, and that was only the first problem. I
heard all about it from my othermother, Tubdu, an
endless source of family history, anecdote, and scan-
dal. "You know," Tubdu told me when I was eleven

or twelve, her eyes shining and her irrepressible, slightly wheezing, almost silent laugh beginning to shake her from the inside out—"you know, she didn't even know women got married? Where she came from, she said, women don't marry."

I could and did correct Tubdu: "Only in her part of it. She told me there's lots of parts of it where they do." I felt obscurely defensive of my mother, though Tubdu spoke without a shadow of malice or contempt; she adored Isako. She had fallen in love with her "the moment I saw her—that black hair! that mouth!"—and simply found it endearingly funny that such a woman could have expected to marry only a man.

"I understand," Tubdu hastened to assure me. "I know—on Terra it's different, their fertility was damaged, they have to think about marrying for children. And they marry in twos, too. Oh, poor Isako! How strange it must have seemed to her! I remember how she looked at me—" And off she went again into what we children called The Great Giggle, her joyous, silent, seismic laughter.

To those unfamiliar with our customs I should explain that on O, a world with a low, stable human population and an ancient climax technology, certain social arrangements are almost universal. The dispersed village, an association of farms, rather than the city or state, is the basic social unit. The population consists of two halves or moieties. A child is born into its mother's moiety, so that all ki'O (except the mountain folk of Ennik) belong either to the Morning People, whose time is from midnight to noon, or the Evening People, whose time is from noon to midnight. The sacred origins and functions of the moieties are recalled in the Discussions and the Plays and in the services at every farm shrine. The original social function of the moiety was probably to structure exogamy into marriage and so

discourage inbreeding in isolated farmholds, since
one can have sex with or marry only a person of the
other moiety. The rule is severely reinforced. Trans-
gressions, which of course occur, are met with
shame, contempt, and ostracism. One's identity as a
Morning or an Evening Person is as deeply and inti-
mately part of oneself as one's gender, and has quite
as much to do with one's sexual life.

A ki'O marriage, called a sedoretu, consists of a
Morning woman and man and an Evening woman
and man; the heterosexual pairs are called Morning
and Evening according to the woman's moiety; the
homosexual pairs are called Day—the two women—
and Night—the two men.

So rigidly structured a marriage, where each of
four people must be sexually compatible with two
of the others while never having sex with the
fourth—clearly this takes some arranging. Making
sedoretu is a major occupation of my people. Experi-
menting is encouraged; foursomes form and dissolve, couples "try on" other couples, mixing and
matching. Brokers, traditionally elderly widowers,
go about among the farmholds of the dispersed villages, arranging meetings, setting up field dances,
serving as universal confidants. Many marriages
begin as a love match of one couple, either homosexual or heterosexual, to which another pair or two
separate people become attached. Many marriages
are brokered or arranged by the village elders from
beginning to end. To listen to the old people under
the village great tree making a sedoretu is like
watching a master game of chess or tidhe. "If that
Evening boy at Erdup were to meet young Tobo during the flour-processing at Gad'd . . ." "Isn't
Hodin'n of the Oto Morning a programmer? They
could use a programmer at Erdup. . . ." The dowry a
prospective bride or groom can offer is their skill, or
their home farm. Otherwise undesired people may

be chosen and honored for the knowledge or the
property they bring to a marriage. The farmhold, in
turn, wants its new members to be agreeable and
useful. There is no end to the making of marriages
on O. I should say that all in all they give as much
satisfaction as any other arrangement to the partici-
pants, and a good deal more to the marriage-makers.

Of course many people never marry. Scholars,
wandering Discussers, itinerant artists and experts,
and specialists in the Centers seldom want to fit
themselves into the massive permanence of a
farmhold sedoretu. Many people attach themselves
to a brother's or sister's marriage as aunt or uncle, a
position with limited, clearly defined responsibilities; they can have sex with either or both spouses of
the other moiety, thus sometimes increasing the
sedoretu from four to seven or eight. Children of
that relationship are called cousins. The children of
one mother are brothers or sisters to one another;
the children of the Morning and the children of the
Evening are germanes. Brothers, sisters, and first
cousins may not marry, but germanes may. In some
less conservative parts of O germane marriages are
looked at askance, but they are common and
respected in my region.

My father was a Morning man of Udan
Farmhold of Derdan'nad Village in the hill region of
the Northwest Watershed of the Saduun River, on
Oket, the smallest of the six continents of O. The village comprises seventy-seven farmholds, in a deeply
rolling, stream-cut region of fields and forests on the
watershed of the Oro, a tributary of the wide Saduun. It is fertile, pleasant country, with views west to
the Coast Range and south to the great floodplains
of the Saduun and the gleam of the sea beyond. The
Oro is a wide, lively, noisy river full of fish and children. I spent my childhood in or on or by the Oro,
which runs through Udan so near the house that

you can hear its voice all night, the rush and hiss of
the water and the deep drumbeats of rocks rolled in
its current. It is shallow and quite dangerous. We all
learned to swim very young in a quiet bay dug out
as a swimming pool, and later to handle rowboats
and kayaks in the swift current full of rocks and
rapids. Fishing was one of the children's responsibilities. I liked to spear the fat, beady-eyed, blue
ochid; I would stand heroic on a slippery boulder in
midstream, the long spear poised to strike. I was
good at it. But my germane Isidri, while I was pranc-
ing about with my spear, would slip into the water
and catch six or seven ochid with her bare hands.
She could catch eels and even the darting ei. I never
could do it. "You just sort of move with the water
and get transparent," she said. She could stay under-
water longer than any of us, so long you were sure
she had drowned. "She's too bad to drown," her
mother, Tubdu, proclaimed. "You can't drown really
bad people. They always bob up again."

Tubdu, the Morning wife, had two children with
her husband Kap: Isidri, a year older than me, and
Suudi, three years younger. Children of the Morning,
they were my germanes, as was Cousin Had'd,
Tubdu's son with Kap's brother Uncle Tobo. On the
Evening side there were two children, myself and my
younger sister. She was named Koneko, an old name
in Oket, which has also a meaning in my mother's
Terran language: "kitten," the young of the wonderful animal "cat" with the round back and the round
eyes. Koneko, four years younger than me, was
indeed round and silky like a baby animal, but her
eyes were like my mother's, long, with lids that went
up towards the temple, like the soft sheaths of flowers before they open. She staggered around after me,
calling, "Deo! Deo! Wait!"—while I ran after fleet, fear-
less, ever-vanishing Isidri, calling, "Sidi! Sidi! Wait!"

When we were older, Isidri and I were inseparable

companions, while Suudi, Koneko, and Cousin
Had'd made a trinity, usually coated with mud,
splotched with scabs, and in some kind of trouble—
gates left open so the yamas got into the crops, hay
spoiled by being jumped on, fruit stolen, battles
with the children from Drehe Farmhold. "Bad, bad,"
Tubdu would say. "None of 'em will ever drown!"
And she would shake with her silent laughter.

My father Dohedri was a hardworking man,
handsome, silent, and aloof. I think his insistence
on bringing a foreigner into the tight-woven fabric
of village and farm life, conservative and suspicious
and full of old knots and tangles of passions and
jealousies, had added anxiety to a temperament
already serious. Other ki'O had married foreigners,
of course, but almost always in a "foreign marriage," a pairing; and such couples usually lived in
one of the Centers, where all kinds of untraditional
arrangements were common, even (so the village
gossips hissed under the great tree) incestuous cou-
plings between two Morning people! two Evening
people!—Or such pairs would leave O to live on
Hain, or would cut all ties to all homes and become
Mobiles on the NAFAL ships, only touching different worlds at different moments and then off again
into an endless future with no past.

None of this would do for my father, a man root-
ed to the knees in the dirt of Udan Farmhold. He
brought his beloved to his home, and persuaded the
Evening People of Derdan'nad to take her into their
moiety, in a ceremony so rare and ancient that a
Caretaker had to come by ship and train from
Noratan to perform it. Then he had persuaded
Tubdu to join the sedoretu. As regards her Day marriage, this was no trouble at all, as soon as Tubdu
met my mother; but it presented some difficulty as
regards her Morning marriage. Kap and my father
had been lovers for years; Kap was the obvious and

willing candidate to complete the sedoretu; but
Tubdu did not like him. Kap's long love for my
father led him to woo Tubdu earnestly and well, and
she was far too good-natured to hold out against the
interlocking wishes of three people, plus her own
lively desire for Isako. She always found Kap a boring husband, I think; but his younger brother, Uncle
Tobo, was a bonus. And Tubdu's relation to my
mother was infinitely tender, full of honor, of deli-
cacy, of restraint. Once my mother spoke of it. "She
knew how strange it all was to me," she said. "She
knows how strange it all is."

"This world? our ways?" I asked.

My mother shook her head very slightly. "Not so
much that," she said in her quiet voice with the
faint foreign accent. "But men and women, women
and women, together—love—It is always very
strange. Nothing you know ever prepares you.
Ever."

The saying is, "a marriage is made by Day," that
is, the relationship of the two women makes or
breaks it. Though my mother and father loved each
other deeply, it was a love always on the edge of
pain, never easy. I have no doubt that the radiant
childhood we had in that household was founded
on the unshakable joy and strength Isako and
Tubdu found in each other.

So, then: twelve-year-old Isidri went off on the
suntrain to school at Herhot, our district educa-
tional Center, and I wept aloud, standing in the
morning sunlight in the dust of Derdan'nad Station. My friend, my playmate, my life was gone. I
was bereft, deserted, alone forever. Seeing her
mighty eleven-year-old elder brother weeping,
Koneko set up a howl too, tears rolling down her
cheeks in dusty balls like raindrops on a dirt road.
She threw her arms about me, roaring, "Hideo!
She'll come back! She'll come back!"

I have never forgotten that. I can hear her
hoarse little voice, and feel her arms round me and
the hot morning sunlight on my neck.

By afternoon we were all swimming in the Oro,
Koneko and I and Suudi and Had'd. As their elder, I
resolved on a course of duty and stern virtue, and led
the troop off to help Second-Cousin Topi at the irrigation control station, until she drove us away like a
swarm of flies, saying, "Go help somebody else and
let me get some work done!" We went and built a
mud palace.

So, then: a year later, twelve-year-old Hideo and
thirteen-year-old Isidri went off on the suntrain to
school, leaving Koneko on the dusty siding, not in
tears, but silent, the way our mother was silent
when she grieved.

I loved school. I know that the first days I was
achingly homesick, but I cannot recall that misery,
buried under my memories of the full, rich years at
Herhot, and later at Ran'n, the Advanced Education
Center, where I studied temporal physics and engineering.

Isidri finished the First Courses at Herhot, took
a year of Second in literature, hydrology, and oenol-
ogy, and went home to Udan Farmhold of
Derdan'nad Village in the hill region of the Northwest Watershed of the Saduun.

The three younger ones all came to school, took a
year or two of Second, and carried their learning
home to Udan. When she was fifteen or sixteen,
Koneko talked of following me to Ran'n; but she was
wanted at home because of her excellence in the dis-
cipline we call "thick planning"—farm management
is the usual translation, but the words have no hint
of the complexity of factors involved in thick planning, ecology politics profit tradition aesthetics
honor and spirit all functioning in an intensely practical and practically invisible balance of preservation

and renewal, like the homeostasis of a vigorous
organism. Our "kitten" had the knack for it, and the
Planners of Udan and Derdan'nad took her into their
councils before she was twenty. But by then, I was
gone.

Every winter of my school years I came back to
the farm for the long holidays. The moment I was
home I dropped school like a book bag and became
pure farm boy overnight—working, swimming, fishing, hiking, putting on Plays and farces in the barn,
going to field dances and house dances all over the
village, falling in and out of love with lovely boys
and girls of the Morning from Derdan'nad and
other villages.

In my last couple of years at Ran'n, my visits
home changed mood. Instead of hiking off all over
the country by day and going to a different dance
every night, I often stayed home. Careful not to fall
in love, I pulled away from my old, dear relationship with Sota of Drehe Farmhold, gradually letting
it lapse, trying not to hurt him. I sat whole hours by
the Oro, a fishing line in my hand, memorizing
the run of the water in a certain place just outside
the entrance to our old swimming bay. There, as the
water rises in clear strands racing towards two
mossy, almost-submerged boulders, it surges and
whirls in spirals, and while some of these spin away,
grow faint, and disappear, one knots itself on a deep
center, becoming a little whirlpool, which spins
slowly downstream until, reaching the quick, bright
race between the boulders, it loosens and unties
itself, released into the body of the river, as another
spiral is forming and knotting itself round a deep
center upstream where the water rises in clear
strands above the boulders. . . . Sometimes that winter the river rose right over the rocks and poured
smooth, swollen with rain; but always it would
drop, and the whirlpools would appear again.

In the winter evenings I talked with my sister and Suudi, serious, long talks by the fire. I watched my mother's beautiful hands work on the embroidery of new curtains for the wide windows of the dining room, which my father had sewn on the four-hundred-year-old sewing machine of Udan. I worked with him on reprogramming the fertilizer systems for the east fields and the yama rotations, according to our thick-planning council's directives. Now and then he and I talked a little, never very much. In the evenings we had music; Cousin Had'd was a drummer, much in demand for dances, who could always gather a group. Or I would play Word-Thief with Tubdu, a game she adored and always lost at because she was so intent to steal my words that she forgot to protect her own. "Got you, got you!" she would cry, and melt into The Great Giggle, seizing my letterblocks with her fat, tapering, brown fingers; and next move I would take all my letters back along with most of hers. "How did you see that?" she would ask, amazed, studying the scattered words. Sometimes my otherfather Kap played with us, methodical, a bit mechanical, with a small smile for both triumph and defeat.

Then I would go up to my room under the eaves, my room of dark wood walls and dark red curtains, the smell of rain coming in the window, the sound of rain on the tiles of the roof. I would lie there in the mild darkness and luxuriate in sorrow, in great, aching, sweet, youthful sorrow for this ancient home that I was going to leave, to lose forever, to sail away from on the dark river of time. For I knew, from my eighteenth birthday on, that I would leave Udan, leave O, and go out to the other worlds. It was my ambition. It was my destiny.

I have not said anything about Isidri, as I described those winter holidays. She was there. She played in the Plays, worked on the farm, went to the dances, sang the choruses, joined the hiking parties, swam in the river in the warm rain with the rest of us. My first winter home from Ran'n, as I swung off the train at Derdan'nad Station, she greeted me with a cry of delight and a great embrace, then broke away with a strange, startled laugh and stood back, a tall, dark, thin girl with an intent, watchful face. She was quite awkward with me that evening. I felt that it was because she had always seen me as a little boy, a child, and now, eighteen and a student at Ran'n, I was a man. I was complacent with Isidri, putting her at her ease, patronizing her. In the days that followed, she remained awkward, laughing inappropriately, never opening her heart to me in the kind of long talks we used to have, and even, I thought, avoiding me. My whole last tenday at home that year, Isidri spent visiting her father's relatives in Sabtodiu Village. I was offended that she had not put off her visit till I was gone.

The next year she was not awkward, but not intimate. She had become interested in religion, attending the shrine daily, studying the Discussions with the elders. She was kind, friendly, busy. I do not remember that she and I ever touched that winter until she kissed me good-bye. Among my people a kiss is not with the mouth; we lay our cheeks together for a moment, or for longer. Her kiss was as light as the touch of a leaf, lingering yet barely perceptible.

My third and last winter home, I told them I was leaving: going to Hain, and that from Hain I wanted to go on farther and forever.

How cruel we are to our parents! All I needed to say was that I was going to Hain. After her half-anguished, half-exultant cry of "I knew it!" my mother said in her usual soft voice, suggesting not stating, "After that, you might come back, for a while." I could have said, "Yes." That was all she asked. Yes, I might come back, for a while. With the impenetrable self-centeredness of youth, which mistakes itself for honesty, I refused to give her what she asked. I took from her the modest hope of seeing me after ten years, and gave her the desolation of believing that when I left she would never see me again. "If I qualify, I want to be a Mobile," I said. I had steeled myself to speak without palliations. I prided myself on my truthfulness. And all the time, though I didn't know it, nor did they, it was not the truth at all. The truth is rarely so simple, though not many truths are as complicated as mine turned out to be.

She took my brutality without the least complaint. She had left her own people, after all. She said that evening, "We can talk by ansible, sometimes, as long as you're on Hain." She said it as if reassuring me, not herself. I think she was remembering how she had said good-bye to her people and boarded the ship on Terra, and when she landed a few seeming hours later on Hain, her mother had been dead for fifty years. She could have talked to Terra on the ansible; but who was there for her to talk to? I did not know that pain, but she did. She took comfort in knowing I would be spared it, for a while.

Everything now was "for a while." Oh, the bitter sweetness of those days! How I enjoyed myself— standing, again, poised on the slick boulder amidst the roaring water, spear raised, the hero! How ready, how willing I was to crush all that long, slow, deep, rich life of Udan in my hand and toss it away!

Only for one moment was I told what I was doing, and then so briefly that I could deny it.

I was down in the boathouse workshop, on the rainy, warm afternoon of a day late in the last month of winter. The constant, hissing thunder of the swollen river was the matrix of my thoughts as I set a new thwart in the little red rowboat we used to fish from, taking pleasure in the task, indulging my anticipatory nostalgia to the full by imagining myself on another planet a hundred years away remembering this hour in the boathouse, the smell of wood and water, the river's incessant roar. A knock at the workshop door. Isidri looked in. The thin, dark, watchful face, the long braid of dark hair, not as black as mine, the intent, clear eyes. "Hideo," she said, "I want to talk to you for a minute."

"Come on in!" I said, pretending ease and gladness, though half-aware that in fact I shrank from talking with Isidri, that I was afraid of her—why?

She perched on the vise bench and watched me work in silence for a little while. I began to say something commonplace, but she spoke: "Do you know why I've been staying away from you?"

Liar, self-protective liar, I said, "Staying away from me?"

At that she sighed. She had hoped I would say I understood, and spare her the rest. But I couldn't. I was lying only in pretending that I hadn't noticed that she had kept away from me. I truly had never, never until she told me, imagined why.

"I found out I was in love with you, winter before last," she said. "I wasn't going to say anything about it because—well, you know. If you'd felt anything like that for me, you'd have known I did. But it wasn't both of us. So there was no good in it. But then, when you told us you're leaving . . . At first I thought, all the more reason to say nothing. But then I thought, that wouldn't be fair. To me, partly. Love has a right to be spoken. And you have a right to know that somebody loves you. That somebody has loved you, could love you. We all need to know that. Maybe it's what we need most. So I wanted to tell you. And because I was afraid you thought I'd kept away from you because I didn't love you, or care about you, you know. It might have looked like that. But it wasn't that." She had slipped down off the table and was at the door.

"Sidi!" I said, her name breaking from me in a strange, hoarse cry, the name only, no words—I had no words. I had no feelings, no compassion, no more nostalgia, no more luxurious suffering. Shocked out of emotion, bewildered, blank, I stood there. Our eyes met. For four or five breaths we stood staring into each other's soul. Then Isidri looked away with a wincing, desolate smile, and slipped out.

I did not follow her. I had nothing to say to her: literally. I felt that it would take me a month, a year, years, to find the words I needed to say to her. I had been so rich, so comfortably complete in myself and my ambition and my destiny, five minutes ago; and now I stood empty, silent, poor, looking at the world I had thrown away.

That ability to look at the truth lasted an hour or so. All my life since I have thought of it as "the hour in the boathouse." I sat on the high bench where Isidri had sat. The rain fell and the river roared and the early night came on. When at last I moved, I turned on a light, and began to try to defend my purpose, my planned future, from the terrible plain reality. I began to build up a screen of emotions and evasions and versions; to look away from what Isidri had shown me; to look away from Isidri's eyes.

By the time I went up to the house for dinner I was in control of myself. By the time I went to bed I was master of my destiny again, sure of my decision, almost able to indulge myself in feeling sorry for Isidri—but not quite. Never did I dishonor her with that. I will say that much for myself. I had had the pity that is self-pity knocked out of me in the hour in the boathouse. When I parted from my family at the

muddy little station in the village, a few days after, I
wept, not luxuriously for them, but for myself, in
honest, hopeless pain. It was too much for me to
bear. I had had so little practice in pain! I said to my
mother, "I will come back. When I finish the
course—six years, maybe seven—I'll come back, I'll
stay a while."

"If your way brings you," she whispered. She
held me close to her, and then released me.

So, then: I have come to the time I chose to
begin my story, when I was twenty-one and left my
home on the ship *Terraces of Darranda* to study at
the Schools on Hain.

Of the journey itself I have no memory whatever. I think I remember entering the ship, yet no
details come to mind, visual or kinetic; I cannot recollect being on the ship. My memory of leaving it is
only of an overwhelming physical sensation, dizziness. I staggered and felt sick, and was so unsteady
on my feet I had to be supported until I had taken
several steps on the soil of Hain.

Troubled by this lapse of consciousness, I asked
about it at the Ekumenical School. I was told that it
is one of the many different ways in which travel at
near- lightspeed affects the mind. To most people it
seems merely that a few hours pass in a kind of perceptual limbo; others have curious perceptions of
space and time and event, which can be seriously
disturbing; a few simply feel they have been asleep
when they "wake up" on arrival. I did not even have
that experience. I had no experience at all. I felt
cheated. I wanted to have felt the voyage, to have
known, in some way, the great interval of space: but
as far as I was concerned, there was no interval. I
was at the spaceport on O, and then I was at Ve Port,
dizzy, bewildered, and at last, when I was able to
believe that I was there, excited.

My studies and work during those years are of

no interest now. I will mention only one event, which may or may not be on record in the ansible reception file at Fourth Beck Tower, EY 21-11-93/1645. (The last time I checked, it was on record in the ansible transmission file at Ran'n, ET date 30-11-93/1645. Urashima's coming and going was on record, too, in the Annals of the Emperors.) 1645 was my first year on Hain. Early in the term I was asked to come to the ansible center, where they explained that they had received a garbled screen transmission, apparently from O, and hoped I could help them reconstitute it. After a date nine days later than the date of reception, it read:

> *les oku n hide problem netru emit it hurt di it*
> *may not be salv devir*

The words were gapped and fragmented. Some were standard Hainish, but *oku* and *netru* mean "north" and "symmetrical" in Sio, my native language. The ansible centers on O had reported no record of the transmission, but the Receivers thought the message might be from O because of these two words and because the Hainish phrase "it may not be salvageable" occurred in a transmission received almost simultaneously from one of the Stabiles on O, concerning a wave-damaged desalinization plant. "We call this a creased message," the Receiver told me, when I confessed I could make nothing of it and asked how often ansible messages came through so garbled. "Not often, fortunately. We can't be certain where or when they originated, or will originate. They may be effects of a double field—interference phenomena, perhaps. One of my colleagues here calls them ghost messages."

Instantaneous transmission had always fascinated me, and though I was then only a beginner in ansible principle, I developed this fortuitous acquaintance with the Receivers into a friendship with several of them. And I took all the courses in ansible theory that were offered.

When I was in my final year in the school of temporal physics, and considering going on to the Cetian Worlds for further study—after my promised visit home, which seemed sometimes a remote, irrelevant daydream and sometimes a yearning and yet fearful need—the first reports came over the ansible from Anarres of the new theory of transilience. Not only information, but matter, bodies, people might be transported from place to place without lapse of time. "Churten technology" was suddenly a reality, although a very strange reality, an implausible fact.

I was crazy to work on it. I was about to go promise my soul and body to the School if they would let me work on churten theory when they came and asked me if I'd consider postponing my training as a Mobile for a year or so to work on churten theory. Judiciously and graciously, I consented. I celebrated all over town that night. I remember showing all my friends how to dance the fen'n, and I remember setting off fireworks in the Great Plaza of the Schools, and I think I remember singing under the Director's windows, a little before dawn. I remember what I felt like next day, too; but it didn't keep me from dragging myself over to the Ti-Phy building to see where they were installing the Churten Field Laboratory.

Ansible transmission is, of course, enormously expensive, and I had only been able to talk to my family twice during my years on Hain; but my friends in the ansible center would occasionally "ride" a screen message for me on a transmission to O. I sent a message thus to Ran'n to be posted on to the First Sedoretu of Udan Farmhold of Derdan'nad

Village of the hill district of the Northwest Watershed of the Saduun, Oket, on O, telling them that "although this research will delay my visit home, it may save me four years' travel." The flippant message revealed my guilty feeling; but we did really think then that we would have the technology within a few months.

The Field Laboratories were soon moved out to Ve Port, and I went with them. The joint work of the Cetian and Hainish churten research teams in those first three years was a succession of triumphs, postponements, promises, defeats, breakthroughs, setbacks, all happening so fast that anybody who took a week off was out-of-date. "Clarity hiding mystery," Gvonesh called it. Every time it all came clear it all grew more mysterious. The theory was beautiful and maddening. The experiments were exciting and inscrutable. The technology worked best when it was most preposterous. Four years went by in that laboratory like no time at all, as they say.

I had now spent ten years on Hain and Ve, and was thirty-one. On O, four years had passed while my NAFAL ship passed a few minutes of dilated time going to Hain, and four more would pass while I returned: so when I returned I would have been gone eighteen of their years. My parents were all still alive. It was high time for my promised visit home.

But though churten research had hit a frustrating setback in the Spring Snow Paradox, a problem the Cetians thought might be insoluble, I couldn't stand the thought of being eight years out-of-date when I got back to Hain. What if they broke the paradox? It was bad enough knowing I must lose four years going to O. Tentatively, not too hopefully, I proposed to the Director that I carry some experimental materials with me to O and set up a fixed double-field auxiliary to the ansible link between Ve

Port and Ran'n. Thus I could stay in touch with Ve, as Ve stayed in touch with Urras and Anarres; and the fixed ansible link might be preparatory to a churten link. I remember I said, "If you break the paradox, we might eventually send some mice."

To my surprise my idea caught on; the temporal engineers wanted a receiving field. Even our Director, who could be as brilliantly inscrutable as churten theory itself, said it was a good idea. "Mouses, bugs, gholes, who knows what we send you?" she said.

So, then: when I was thirty-one years old I left Ve Port on the NAFAL transport *Lady of Sorra* and returned to O. This time I experienced the near-lightspeed flight the way most people do, as an unnerving interlude in which one cannot think consecutively, read a clockface, or follow a story. Speech and movement become difficult or impossible. Other people appear as unreal half presences, inexplicably there or not there. I did not hallucinate, but everything seemed hallucination. It is like a high fever—confusing, miserably boring, seeming endless, yet very difficult to recall once it is over, as if it were an episode outside one's life, encapsulated. I wonder now if its resemblance to the "churten experience" has yet been seriously investigated.

I went straight to Ran'n, where I was given rooms in the New Quadrangle, fancier than my old student room in the Shrine Quadrangle, and some nice lab space in Tower Hall to set up an experimental transilience field station. I got in touch with my family right away and talked to all my parents; my mother had been ill, but was fine now, she said. I told them I would be home as soon as I had got things going at Ran'n. Every tenday I called again and talked to them and said I'd be along very soon now. I was genuinely very busy, having to catch up the lost four years and to learn Gvonesh's solution

to the Spring Snow Paradox. It was, fortunately, the
only major advance in theory. Technology had
advanced a good deal. I had to retrain myself, and to
train my assistants almost from scratch. I had had
an idea about an aspect of double-field theory that I
wanted to work out before I left. Five months went
by before I called them up and said at last, "I'll be
there tomorrow." And when I did so, I realized that
all along I had been afraid.

I don't know if I was afraid of seeing them after
eighteen years, of the changes, the strangeness, or if
it was myself I feared.

Eighteen years had made no difference at all
to the hills beside the wide Saduun, the farmlands,
the dusty little station in Derdan'nad, the old, old
houses on the quiet streets. The village great tree
was gone, but its replacement had a pretty wide
spread of shade already. The aviary at Udan had
been enlarged. The yama stared haughtily, timidly
at me across the fence. A road gate that I had hung
on my last visit home was decrepit, needing its post
reset and new hinges, but the weeds that grew
beside it were the same dusty, sweet-smelling summer weeds. The tiny dams of the irrigation runnels
made their multiple, soft click and thump as they
closed and opened. Everything was the same, itself.
Timeless, Udan in its dream of work stood over the
river that ran timeless in its dream of movement.

But the faces and bodies of the people waiting
for me at the station in the hot sunlight were not the
same. My mother, forty-seven when I left, was sixty-
five, a beautiful and fragile elderly woman. Tubdu
had lost weight; she looked shrunken and wistful.
My father was still handsome and bore himself
proudly, but his movements were slow and he
scarcely spoke at all. My otherfather Kap, seventy
now, was a precise, fidgety, little old man. They
were still the First Sedoretu of Udan, but the vigor of

the farmhold now lay in the Second and Third Sedoretu.

I knew of all the changes, of course, but being there among them was a different matter from hearing about them in letters and transmissions. The old house was much fuller than it had been when I lived there. The south wing had been reopened, and children ran in and out of its doors and across courtyards that in my childhood had been silent and ivied and mysterious.

My sister Koneko was now four years older than I instead of four years younger. She looked very like my early memory of my mother. As the train drew in to Derdan'nad Station, she had been the first of them I recognized, holding up a child of three or four and saying, "Look, look, it's your Uncle Hideo!"

The Second Sedoretu had been married for eleven years: Koneko and Isidri, sister-germanes, were the partners of the Day. Koneko's husband was my old friend Sota, a Morning man of Drehe Farmhold. Sota and I had loved each other dearly when we were adolescents, and I had been grieved to grieve him when I left. When I heard that he and Koneko were in love I had been very surprised, so self-centered am I, but at least I am not jealous: it pleased me very deeply. Isidri's husband, a man nearly twenty years older than herself, named Hedran, had been a traveling scholar of the Discussions. Udan had given him hospitality, and his visits had led to the marriage. He and Isidri had no children. Sota and Koneko had two Evening children, a boy of ten called Murmi, and Lasako, Little Isako, who was four.

The Third Sedoretu had been brought to Udan by Suudi, my brother-germane, who had married a woman from Aster Village; their Morning pair also came from farmholds of Aster. There were six children in that sedoretu. A cousin whose sedoretu at

Ekke had broken had also come to live at Udan with her two children; so the coming and going and dressing and undressing and washing and slamming and running and shouting and weeping and laughing and eating was prodigious. Tubdu would sit at work in the sunny kitchen courtyard and watch a wave of children pass. "Bad!" she would cry. "They'll never drown, not a one of 'em!" And she would shake with silent laughter that became a wheezing cough.

My mother, who had after all been a Mobile of the Ekumen, and had traveled from Terra to Hain and from Hain to O, was impatient to hear about my research. "What is it, this churtening? How does it work, what does it do? Is it an ansible for matter?"

"That's the idea," I said. "Transilience: instantaneous transference of being from one s-tc point to another."

"No interval?"

"No interval."

Isako frowned. "It sounds wrong," she said. "Explain."

I had forgotten how direct my soft-spoken mother could be; I had forgotten that she was an intellectual. I did my best to explain the incomprehensible.

"So," she said at last, "you don't really understand how it works."

"No. Nor even what it does. Except that—as a rule—when the field is in operation, the mice in Building One are instantaneously in Building Two, perfectly cheerful and unharmed. Inside their cage, if we remembered to keep their cage inside the initiating churten field. We used to forget. Loose mice everywhere."

"What's *mice?*" said a little Morning boy of the Third Sedoretu, who had stopped to listen to what sounded like a story.

"Ah," I said in a laugh, surprised. I had forgotten

that at Udan mice were unknown, and rats were fanged, demon enemies of the painted cat. "Tiny, pretty, furry animals," I said, "that come from Grandmother Isako's world. They are friends of scientists. They have traveled all over the Known Worlds."

"In tiny little spaceships?" the child said hopefully.

"In large ones, mostly," I said. He was satisfied, and went away.

"Hideo," said my mother, in the terrifying way women have of passing without interval from one subject to another because they have them all present in their mind at once, "you haven't found any kind of relationship?"

I shook my head, smiling.

"None at all?"

"A man from Alterra and I lived together for a couple of years," I said. "It was a good friendship; but he's a Mobile now. And . . . oh, you know . . . people here and there. Just recently, at Ran'n, I've been with a very nice woman from East Oket."

"I hoped, if you intend to be a Mobile, that you might make a couple-marriage with another Mobile. It's easier, I think," she said. Easier than what? I thought, and knew the answer before I asked.

"Mother, I doubt now that I'll travel farther than Hain. This churten business is too interesting; I want to be in on it. And if we do learn to control the technology, you know, then travel will be nothing. There'll be no need for the kind of sacrifice you made. Things will be different. Unimaginably different! You could go to Terra for an hour and come back here: and only an hour would have passed."

She thought about that. "If you do it, then," she said, speaking slowly, almost shaking with the intensity of comprehension, "you will . . . you will shrink the galaxy—the universe?—to . . . " and she held up her left hand, thumb and fingers all drawn together to a point.

I nodded. "A mile or a light-year will be the same. There will be no distance."

"It can't be right," she said after a while. "To have event without interval . . . Where is the dancing? Where is the way? I don't think you'll be able to control it, Hideo." She smiled. "But of course you must try."

And after that we talked about who was coming to the field dance at Drehe tomorrow.

I did not tell my mother that I had invited Tasi, the nice woman from East Oket, to come to Udan with me and that she had refused, had, in fact, gently informed me that she thought this was a good time for us to part. Tasi was tall, with a braid of dark hair, not coarse, bright black like mine but soft, fine, dark, like the shadows in a forest. A typical ki'O woman, I thought. She had deflated my protestations of love skillfully and without shaming me. "I think you're in love with somebody, though," she said. "Somebody on Hain, maybe. Maybe the man from Alterra you told me about?" No, I said. No, I'd never been in love. I wasn't capable of an intense relationship, that was clear by now. I'd dreamed too long of traveling the galaxy with no attachments anywhere, and then worked too long in the churten lab, married to a damned theory that couldn't find its technology. No room for love, no time.

But why had I wanted to bring Tasi home with me?

Tall but no longer thin, a woman of forty, not a girl, not typical, not comparable, not like anyone anywhere, Isidri had greeted me quietly at the door of the house. Some farm emergency had kept her from coming to the village station to meet me. She was wearing an old smock and leggings like any field worker, and her hair, dark beginning to grey, was in a rough braid. As she stood in that wide doorway of polished wood she was Udan itself, the body and soul of that thirty-century-old farmhold, its continuity, its life. All my childhood was in her hands, and she held them out to me.

"Welcome home, Hideo," she said, with a smile as radiant as the summer light on the river. As she brought me in, she said, "I cleared the kids out of your old room. I thought you'd like to be there— would you?" Again she smiled, and I felt her warmth, the solar generosity of a woman in the prime of life, married, settled, rich in her work and being. I had not needed Tasi as a defense. I had nothing to fear from Isidri. She felt no rancor, no embarrassment. She had loved me when she was young, another person. It would be altogether inappropriate for me to feel embarrassment, or shame, or anything but the old affectionate loyalty of the years when we played and worked and fished and dreamed together, children of Udan.

So, then: I settled down in my old room under the tiles. There were new curtains, rust and brown. I found a stray toy under the chair, in the closet, as if I as a child had left my playthings there and found them now. At fourteen, after my entry ceremony in the shrine, I had carved my name on the deep window jamb among the tangled patterns of names and symbols that had been cut into it for centuries. I looked for it now. There had been some additions. Beside my careful, clear *Hideo*, surrounded by my ideogram, the cloudflower, a younger child had hacked a straggling *Dohedri*, and nearby was carved a delicate three-roofs ideogram. The sense of being a bubble in Udan's river, a moment in the permanence of life in this house on this land on this quiet world, was almost crushing, denying my identity, and profoundly reassuring, confirming my identity. Those nights of my visit home I slept as I had not slept for years, lost, drowned in the waters of sleep and darkness, and woke to the summer mornings as if reborn, very hungry.

The children were still all under twelve, going to school at home. Isidri, who taught them literature and religion and was the school planner, invited me to tell them about Hain, about NAFAL travel, about temporal physics, whatever I pleased. Visitors to ki'O farmholds are always put to use. Evening-Uncle Hideo became rather a favorite among the children, always good for hitching up the yama-cart or taking them fishing in the big boat, which they couldn't yet handle, or telling a story about his magic mice who could be in two places at the same time. I asked them if Evening-Grandmother Isako had told them about the painted cat who came alive and killed the demon rats—"And his mouf was all BLUGGY in the morning!" shouted Lasako, her eyes shining. But they didn't know the tale of Urashima.

"Why haven't you told them 'The Fisherman of the Inland Sea'?" I asked my mother.

She smiled and said, "Oh, that was your story. You always wanted it."

I saw Isidri's eyes on us, clear and tranquil, yet watchful still.

I knew my mother had had repair and healing to her heart a year before, and I asked Isidri later, as we supervised some work the older children were doing, "Has Isako recovered, do you think?"

"She seems wonderfully well since you came. I don't know. It's damage from her childhood, from the poisons in the Terran biosphere; they say her immune system is easily depressed. She was very patient about being ill. Almost too patient."

"And Tubdu—does she need new lungs?"

"Probably. All four of them are getting older, and stubborner. . . . But you look at Isako for me. See if you see what I mean."

I tried to observe my mother. After a few days I reported back that she seemed energetic and decisive, even imperative, and that I hadn't seen much of the patient endurance that worried Isidri. She laughed.

"Isako told me once," she said, "that a mother is connected to her child by a very fine, thin cord, like the umbilical cord, that can stretch light-years without any difficulty. I asked her if it was painful, and she said, 'Oh, no, it's just there, you know, it stretches and stretches and never breaks.' It seems to me it must be painful. But I don't know. I have no child, and I've never been more than two days' travel from my mothers." She smiled and said in her soft, deep voice, "I think I love Isako more than anyone, more even than my mother, more even than Koneko. . . ."

Then she had to show one of Suudi's children how to reprogram the timer on the irrigation control. She was the hydrologist for the village and the oenologist for the farm. Her life was thick-planned, very rich in necessary work and wide relationships, a serene and steady succession of days, seasons, years. She swam in life as she had swum in the river, like a fish, at home. She had borne no child, but all the children of the farmhold were hers. She and Koneko were as deeply attached as their mothers had been. Her relation with her rather fragile, scholarly husband seemed peaceful and respectful. I thought his Night marriage with my old friend Sota might be the stronger sexual link, but Isidri clearly admired and depended on his intellectual and spiritual guidance. I thought his teaching a bit dry and disputatious; but what did I know about religion? I had not given worship for years, and felt strange, out of place, even in the home shrine. I felt strange, out of place, in my home. I did not acknowledge it to myself.

I was conscious of the month as pleasant,

uneventful, even a little boring. My emotions were mild and dull. The wild nostalgia, the romantic sense of standing on the brink of my destiny, all that was gone with the Hideo of twenty-one. Though now the youngest of my generation, I was a grown man, knowing his way, content with his work, past emotional self-indulgence. I wrote a little poem for the house album about the peacefulness of following a chosen course. When I had to go, I embraced and kissed everyone, dozens of soft or harsh cheek-touches. I told them that if I stayed on O, as it seemed I might be asked to do for a year or so, I would come back next winter for another visit. On the train going back through the hills to Ran'n, I thought with a complacent gravity how I might return to the farm next winter, finding them all just the same; and how, if I came back after another eighteen years or even longer, some of them would be gone and some would be new to me and yet it would be always my home, Udan with its wide dark roofs riding time like a dark-sailed ship. I always grow poetic when I am lying to myself.

I got back to Ran'n, checked in with my people at the lab in Tower Hall, and had dinner with colleagues, good food and drink—I brought them a bottle of wine from Udan, for Isidri was making splendid wines, and had given me a case of the fifteen-year-old Kedun. We talked about the latest breakthrough in churten technology, "continuous-field sending," reported from Anarres just yesterday on the ansible. I went to my rooms in the New Quadrangle through the summer night, my head full of physics, read a little, and went to bed. I turned out the light and darkness filled me as it filled the room. Where was I? Alone in a room among strangers. As I had been for ten years and would always be. On one planet or another, what did it matter? Alone, part of nothing, part of no one. Udan was not my home. I

had no home, no people. I had no future, no destiny,
any more than a bubble of foam or a whirlpool in a
current has a destiny. It is and it isn't. Nothing
more.

I turned the light on because I could not bear
the darkness, but the light was worse. I sat huddled
up in the bed and began to cry. I could not stop crying. I became frightened at how the sobs racked and
shook me till I was sick and weak and still could not
stop sobbing. After a long time I calmed myself
gradually by clinging to an imagination, a childish
idea: in the morning I would call Isidri and talk to
her, telling her that I needed instruction in religion,
that I wanted to give worship at the shrines again,
but it had been so long, and I had never listened to
the Discussions, but now I needed to, and I would
ask her, Isidri, to help me. So, holding fast to that, I
could at last stop the terrible sobbing and lie spent,
exhausted, until the day came.

I did not call Isidri. In daylight the thought
which had saved me from the dark seemed foolish;
and I thought if I called her she would ask advice of
her husband, the religious scholar. But I knew I
needed help. I went to the shrine in the Old School
and gave worship. I asked for a copy of the First Discussions, and read it. I joined a Discussion group,
and we read and talked together. My religion is god-
less, argumentative, and mystical. The name of our
world is the first word of its first prayer. For human
beings its vehicle is the human voice and mind. As I
began to rediscover it, I found it quite as strange as
churten theory and in some respects complemen-
tary to it. I knew, but had never understood, that
Cetian physics and religion are aspects of one
knowledge. I wondered if all physics and religion
are aspects of one knowledge.

At night I never slept well and often could not
sleep at all. After the bountiful tables of Udan, col-

lege food seemed poor stuff; I had no appetite. But our work, my work went well—wonderfully well.

"No more mouses," said Gvonesh on the voice ansible from Hain. "Peoples."

"What people?" I demanded.

"Me," said Gvonesh.

So our Director of Research churtened from one corner of Laboratory One to another, and then from Building One to Building Two—vanishing in one laboratory and appearing in the other, smiling, in the same instant, in no time.

"What did it feel like?" they asked, of course, and Gvonesh answered, of course, "Like nothing."

Many experiments followed; mice and gholes churtened halfway around Ve and back; robot crews churtened from Anarres to Urras, from Hain to Ve, and then from Anarres to Ve, twenty-two light-years. So, then, eventually the *Shoby* and her crew of ten human beings churtened into orbit around a miserable planet seventeen light-years from Ve and returned (but words that imply coming and going, that imply distance traveled, are not appropriate) thanks only to their intelligent use of entrainment, rescuing themselves from a kind of chaos of dissolution, a death by unreality, that horrified us all. Experiments with high-intelligence life-forms came to a halt.

"The rhythm is wrong," Gvonesh said on the ansible (she said it "rithkhom.") For a moment I thought of my mother saying, "It can't be right to have event without interval." What else had Isako said? Something about dancing. But I did not want to think about Udan. I did not think about Udan. When I did I felt, far down deeper inside me than my bones, the knowledge of being no one, no where, and a shaking like a frightened animal.

My religion reassured me that I was part of the Way, and my physics absorbed my despair in work.

Experiments, cautiously resumed, succeeded beyond hope. The Terran Dalzul and his psychophysics took everyone at the research station on Ve by storm; I am sorry I never met him. As he predicted, using the continuity field he churtened without a hint of trouble, alone, first locally, then from Ve to Hain, then the great jump to Tadkla and back. From the second journey to Tadkla, his three companions returned without him. He died on that far world. It did not seem to us in the laboratories that his death was in any way caused by the churten field or by what had come to be known as "the churten experience," though his three companions were not so sure.

"Maybe Dalzul was right. One people at a time," said Gvonesh; and she made herself again the subject, the "ritual animal," as the Hainish say, of the next experiment. Using continuity technology she churtened right round Ve in four skips, which took thirty-two seconds because of the time needed to set up the coordinates. We had taken to calling the noninterval in time/real interval in space a "skip." It sounded light, trivial. Scientists like to trivialize.

I wanted to try the improvement to double-field stability that I had been working on ever since I came to Ran'n. It was time to give it a test; my patience was short, life was too short to fiddle with figures forever. Talking to Gvonesh on the ansible I said, "I'll skip over to Ve Port. And then back here to Ran'n. I promised a visit to my home farm this winter." Scientists like to trivialize.

"You still got that wrinkle in your field?" Gvonesh asked. "Some kind, you know, like a fold?"

"It's ironed out, ammar," I assured her.

"Good, fine," said Gvonesh, who never questioned what one said. "Come."

So, then: we set up the fields in a constant stable churten link with ansible connection; and I was standing inside a chalked circle in the Churten Field Laboratory of Ran'n Center on a late autumn afternoon and standing inside a chalked circle in the Churten Research Station Field Laboratory in Ve Port on a late summer day at a distance of 4.2 light-years and no interval of time.

"Feel nothing?" Gvonesh inquired, shaking my hand heartily. "Good fellow, good fellow, welcome, ammar, Hideo. Good to see. No wrinkle, hah?"

I laughed with the shock and queerness of it, and gave Gvonesh the bottle of Udan Kedun '49 that I had picked up a moment ago from the laboratory table on O.

I had expected, if I arrived at all, to churten promptly back again, but Gvonesh and others wanted me on Ve for a while for discussions and tests of the field. I think now that the Director's extraordinary intuition was at work; the "wrinkle," the "fold" in the Tiokunan'n Field still bothered her. "Is unaesthetical," she said.

"But it works," I said.

"It worked," said Gvonesh.

Except to retest my field, to prove its reliability, I had no desire to return to O. I was sleeping somewhat better here on Ve, although food was still unpalatable to me, and when I was not working I felt shaky and drained, a disagreeable reminder of my exhaustion after the night which I tried not to remember when for some reason or other I had cried so much. But the work went very well.

"You got no sex, Hideo?" Gvonesh asked me when we were alone in the Lab one day, I playing with a new set of calculations and she finishing her box lunch.

The question took me utterly aback. I knew it was not as impertinent as Gvonesh's peculiar usage of the language made it sound. But Gvonesh never asked questions like that. Her own sex life was as much a mystery as the rest of her existence. No one had ever heard her mention the word, let alone suggest the act.

When I sat with my mouth open, stumped, she said, "You used to, hah," as she chewed on a cold varvet.

I stammered something. I knew she was not proposing that she and I have sex, but inquiring after my well-being. But I did not know what to say.

"You got some kind of wrinkle in your life, hah," Gvonesh said. "Sorry. Not my business."

Wanting to assure her I had taken no offense I said, as we say on O, "I honor your intent."

She looked directly at me, something she rarely did. Her eyes were clear as water in her long, bony face softened by a fine, thick, colorless down. "Maybe is time you go back to O?" she asked.

"I don't know. The facilities here—"

She nodded. She always accepted what one said. "You read Harraven's report?" she asked, changing one subject for another as quickly and definitively as my mother.

All right, I thought, the challenge was issued. She was ready for me to test my field again. Why not? After all, I could churten to Ran'n and churten right back again to Ve within a minute, if I chose, and if the Lab could afford it. Like ansible transmission, churtening draws essentially on inertial mass, but setting up the field, disinfecting it, and holding it stable in size uses a good deal of local energy. But it was Gvonesh's suggestion, which meant we had the money. I said, "How about a skip over and back?"

"Fine," Gvonesh said. "Tomorrow."

So the next day, on a morning of late autumn, I stood inside a chalked circle in the Field Laboratory on Ve and stood—

A shimmer, a shivering of everything—a missed beat—skipped—

—in darkness. A darkness. A dark room. The lab? A lab—I found the light panel. In the darkness I was sure it was the laboratory on Ve. In the light I saw it was not. I didn't know where it was. I didn't know where I was. It seemed familiar yet I could not place it. What was it? A biology lab? There were specimens, an old subparticle microscope, the maker's ideogram on the battered brass casing, the lyre ideogram. . . . I was on O. In some laboratory in some building of the Center at Ran'n? It smelled like the old buildings of Ran'n, it smelled like a rainy night on O. But how could I have not arrived in the receiving field, the circle carefully chalked on the wood floor of the lab in Tower Hall? The field itself must have moved. An appalling, an impossible thought.

I was alarmed and felt rather dizzy, as if my body had skipped that beat, but I was not yet frightened. I was all right, all here, all the pieces in the right places, and the mind working. A slight spatial displacement? said the mind.

I went out into the corridor. Perhaps I had myself been disoriented and left the Churten Field Laboratory and come to full consciousness somewhere else. But my crew would have been there; where were they? And that would have been hours ago; it should have been just past noon on O when I arrived. A slight temporal displacement? said the mind, working away. I went down the corridor looking for my lab, and that is when it became like one of those dreams in which you cannot find the room which you must find. It was that dream. The building was perfectly familiar: it was Tower Hall, the second floor of Tower, but there was no Churten Lab. All the labs were biology and biophysics, and all were deserted. It was evidently late at night. Nobody around. At last I saw a light under a door and knocked and opened it on a student reading at a library terminal.

"I'm sorry," I said. "I'm looking for the Churten Field Lab—"

"The what lab?"

She had never heard of it, and apologized. "I'm not in Ti Phy, just Bi Phy," she said humbly.

I apologized too. Something was making me shakier, increasing my sense of dizziness and disorientation. Was this the "chaos effect" the crew of the *Shoby* and perhaps the crew of the *Galba* had experienced? Would I begin to see the stars through the walls, or turn around and see Gvonesh here on O?

I asked her what time it was. "I should have got here at noon," I said, though that of course meant nothing to her.

"It's about one," she said, glancing at the clock on the terminal. I looked at it too. It gave the time, the tenday, the month, the year.

"That's wrong," I said.

She looked worried.

"That's not right," I said. "The date. It's not right." But I knew from the steady glow of the numbers on the clock, from the girl's round, worried face, from the beat of my heart, from the smell of the rain, that it was right, that it was an hour after midnight eighteen years ago, that I was here, now, on the day after the day I called "once upon a time" when I began to tell this story.

A major temporal displacement, said the mind, working, laboring.

"I don't belong here," I said, and turned to hurry back to what seemed a refuge, Biology Lab 6, which would be the Churten Field Lab eighteen years from now, as if I could re-enter the field, which had existed or would exist for .004 second.

The girl saw that something was wrong, made me sit down, and gave me a cup of hot tea from her insulated bottle.

"Where are you from?" I asked her, the kind, serious student.

"Herdud Farmhold of Deada Village on the South Watershed of the Saduun," she said.

"I'm from downriver," I said. "Udan of Derdan'nad." I suddenly broke into tears. I managed to control myself, apologized again, drank my tea, and set the cup down. She was not overly troubled by my fit of weeping. Students are intense people, they laugh and cry, they break down and rebuild. She asked if I had a place to spend the night: a perceptive question. I said I did, thanked her, and left.

I did not go back to the biology laboratory, but went downstairs and started to cut through the gardens to my rooms in the New Quadrangle. As I walked the mind kept working; it worked out that somebody else had been/would be in those rooms then/now.

I turned back towards the Shrine Quadrangle, where I had lived my last two years as a student before I left for Hain. If this was in fact, as the clock had indicated, the night after I had left, my room might still be empty and unlocked. It proved to be so, to be as I had left it, the mattress bare, the cycle-basket unemptied.

That was the most frightening moment. I stared at that cyclebasket for a long time before I took a crumpled bit of outprint from it and carefully smoothed it on the desk. It was a set of temporal equations scribbled on my old pocketscreen in my own handwriting, notes from Sedharad's class in Interval, from my last term at Ran'n, day before yesterday, eighteen years ago.

I was now very shaky indeed. You are caught in a chaos field, said the mind, and I believed it. Fear and stress, and nothing to do about it, not till the long night was past. I lay down on the bare bunk-mattress, ready for the stars to burn through the walls and my eyelids if I shut them. I meant to try and plan what I should do in the morning, if there was a morning. I fell asleep instantly and slept like a stone till broad daylight, when I woke up on the bare bed in the familiar room, alert, hungry, and without a moment of doubt as to who or where or when I was.

I went down into the village for breakfast. I didn't want to meet any colleagues—no, fellow students—who might know me and say, "Hideo! What are you doing here? You left on the *Terraces of Darranda* yesterday!"

I had little hope they would not recognize me. I was thirty-one now, not twenty-one, much thinner and not as fit as I had been; but my half-Terran features were unmistakable. I did not want to be recognized, to have to try to explain. I wanted to get out of Ran'n. I wanted to go home.

O is a good world to time-travel in. Things don't change. Our trains run on the same schedule to the same places for centuries. We sign for payment and pay in contracted barter or cash monthly, so I did not have to produce mysterious coins from the future. I signed at the station and took the morning train to Saduun Delta.

The little suntrain glided through the plains and hills of the South Watershed and then the Northwest Watershed, following the ever-widening river, stopping at each village. I got off in the late afternoon at the station in Derdan'nad. Since it was very early spring, the station was muddy, not dusty.

I walked out the road to Udan. I opened the road gate that I had rehung a few days/eighteen years ago; it moved easily on its new hinges. That gave me a little gleam of pleasure. The she-yamas were all in the nursery pasture. Birthing would start any day; their woolly sides stuck out, and they moved like sailboats in a slow breeze, turning their elegant, scornful heads to look distrustfully at me as I

passed. Rain clouds hung over the hills. I crossed the
Oro on the humpbacked wooden bridge. Four or
five great blue ochid hung in a back-water by the
bridgefoot; I stopped to watch them; if I'd had a
spear . . . The clouds drifted overhead trailing a fine,
faint drizzle. I strode on. My face felt hot and stiff as
the cool rain touched it. I followed the river road
and saw the house come into view, the dark, wide
roofs low on the tree-crowned hill. I came past the
aviary and the collectors, past the irrigation center,
under the avenue of tall bare trees, up the steps of
the deep porch, to the door, the wide door of Udan.
I went in.

Tubdu was crossing the hall—not the woman I
had last seen, in her sixties, grey-haired and tired
and fragile, but Tubdu of The Great Giggle, Tubdu at
forty-five, fat and rosy-brown and brisk, crossing the
hall with short, quick steps, stopping, looking at me
at first with mere recognition, there's Hideo, then
with puzzlement, is that Hideo? and then with
shock—that can't be Hideo!

"Ombu," I said, the baby word for othermother,
"Ombu, it's me, Hideo, don't worry, it's all right, I
came back." I embraced her, pressed my cheek to
hers.

"But, but—" She held me off, looked up at my face.
"But what has happened to you, darling boy?" she
cried, and then, turning, called out in a high voice,
"Isako! Isako!"

When my mother saw me she thought, of course,
that I had not left on the ship to Hain, that my
courage or my intent had failed me; and in her first
embrace there was an involuntary reserve, a with-
holding. Had I thrown away the destiny for which I
had been so ready to throw away everything else? I
knew what was in her mind. I laid my cheek to hers
and whispered, "I did go, mother, and I came back.
I'm thirty-one years old. I came back—"

She held me away a little just as Tubdu had done, and saw my face. "Oh Hideo!" she said, and held me to her with all her strength. "My dear, my dear!"

We held each other in silence, till I said at last, "I need to see Isidri."

My mother looked up at me intently but asked no questions. "She's in the shrine, I think."

"I'll be right back."

I left her and Tubdu side by side and hurried through the halls to the central room, in the oldest part of the house, rebuilt seven centuries ago on the foundations that go back three thousand years. The walls are stone and clay, the roof is thick glass, curved. It is always cool and still there. Books line the walls, the Discussions, the discussions of the Discussions, poetry, texts and versions of the Plays; there are drums and whispersticks for meditation and ceremony; the small, round pool which is the shrine itself wells up from clay pipes and brims its blue-green basin, reflecting the rainy sky above the skylight. Isidri was there. She had brought in fresh boughs for the vase beside the shrine, and was kneeling to arrange them.

I went straight to her and said, "Isidri, I came back. Listen—"

Her face was utterly open, startled, scared, defenseless, the soft, thin face of a woman of twenty-two, the dark eyes gazing into me.

"Listen, Isidri: I went to Hain, I studied there, I worked on a new kind of temporal physics, a new theory—transilience—I spent ten years there. Then we began experiments, I was in Ran'n and crossed over to the Hainish system in no time, using that technology, in no time, you understand me, literally, like the ansible—not at lightspeed, not faster than light, but in no time. In one place and in another place instantaneously, you understand? And it went fine, it worked, but coming back there was . . . there was a fold, a crease, in my field. I was in the same place in a different time. I came back eighteen of your years, ten of mine. I came back to the day I left, but I didn't leave, I came back, I came back to you."

I was holding her hands, kneeling to face her as she knelt by the silent pool. She searched my face with her watchful eyes, silent. On her cheekbone there was a fresh scratch and a little bruise; a branch had lashed her as she gathered the evergreen boughs.

"Let me come back to you," I said in a whisper.

She touched my face with her hand. "You look so tired," she said. "Hideo . . . Are you all right?"

"Yes," I said. "Oh, yes. I'm all right."

And there my story, so far as it has any interest to the Ekumen or to research in transilience, comes to an end. I have lived now for eighteen years as a farmholder of Udan Farm of Derdan'nad Village of the hill region of the Northwest Watershed of the Saduun, on Oket, on O. I am fifty years old. I am the Morning husband of the Second Sedoretu of Udan; my wife is Isidri; my Night marriage is to Sota of Drehe, whose Evening wife is my sister Koneko. My children of the Morning with Isidri are Latubdu and Tadri; the Evening children are Murmi and Lasako. But none of this is of much interest to the Stabiles of the Ekumen.

My mother, who had had some training in temporal engineering, asked for my story, listened to it carefully, and accepted it without question; so did Isidri. Most of the people of my farmhold chose a simpler and far more plausible story, which explained everything fairly well, even my severe loss of weight and ten-year age gain overnight. At the very last moment, just before the space ship left, they said, Hideo decided not to go to the Ekumenical School on Hain after all. He came back to Udan, because he was in love with Isidri. But it had made him quite ill, because it was a very hard decision and he was very much in love.

Maybe that is indeed the true story. But Isidri and Isako chose a stranger truth.

Later, when we were forming our sedoretu, Sota asked me for that truth. "You aren't the same man, Hideo, though you are the man I always loved," he said. I told him why, as best I could. He was sure that Koneko would understand it better than he could, and indeed she listened gravely, and asked several keen questions which I could not answer.

I did attempt to send a message to the temporal physics department of the Ekumenical Schools on Hain. I had not been home long before my mother, with her strong sense of duty and her obligation to the Ekumen, became insistent that I do so.

"Mother," I said, "what can I tell them? They haven't invented churten theory yet!"

"Apologize for not coming to study, as you said you would. And explain it to the Director, the Anarresti woman. Maybe she would understand."

"Even Gvonesh doesn't know about churten yet. They'll begin telling her about it on the ansible from Urras and Anarres about three years from now. Anyhow, Gvonesh didn't know me the first couple of years I was there." The past tense was inevitable but ridiculous; it would have been more accurate to say, "she won't know me the first couple of years I won't be there."

Or *was* I there on Hain, now? That paradoxical idea of two simultaneous existences on two different worlds disturbed me exceedingly. It was one of the points Koneko had asked about. No matter how I discounted it as impossible under every law of temporality, I could not keep from imagining that it was possible, that another I was living on Hain, and would come to Udan in eighteen years and meet myself. After all, my present existence was also and equally impossible.

When such notions haunted and troubled me I learned to replace them with a different image: the little whorls of water that slid down between the two big rocks, where the current ran strong, just above the swimming bay in the Oro. I would imagine those whirlpools forming and dissolving, or I would go down to the river and sit and watch them. And they seemed to hold a solution to my question, to dissolve it as they endlessly dissolved and formed.

But my mother's sense of duty and obligation was unmoved by such trifles as a life impossibly lived twice.

"You should try to tell them," she said.

She was right. If my double transilience field had established itself permanently, it was a matter of real importance to temporal science, not only to myself. So I tried. I borrowed a staggering sum in cash from the farm reserves, went up to Ran'n, bought a five-thousand-word ansible screen transmission, and sent a message to my director of studies at the Ekumenical School, trying to explain why, after being accepted at the School, I had not arrived—if in fact I had not arrived.

I take it that this was the "creased message" or "ghost" they asked me to try to interpret, my first year there. Some of it is gibberish, and some words probably came from the other, nearly simultaneous transmission, but parts of my name are in it, and other words may be fragments or reversals from my long message—problem, churten, return, arrived, time.

It is interesting, I think, that at the ansible center the Receivers used the word "creased" for a temporally disturbed transilient, as Gvonesh would use it for the anomaly, the "wrinkle" in my churten field. In fact, the ansible field was meeting a resonance resistance, caused by the ten-year anomaly in the churten field, which did fold the message back into itself, crumple it up, inverting and erasing. At that point, within the implication of the Tiokunan'n Double Field, my existence on O as I sent the message was simultaneous with my existence on Hain when the message was received. There was an I who sent and an I who received. Yet, so long as the encapsulated field anomaly existed, the simultaneity was literally a point, an instant, a crossing without further implication in either the ansible or the churten field.

An image for the churten field in this case might be a river winding in its floodplain, winding in deep, redoubling curves, folding back upon itself so closely that at last the current breaks through the double banks of the S and runs straight, leaving a whole reach of the water aside as a curving lake, cut off from the current, unconnected. In this analogy, my ansible message would have been the one link, other than my memory, between the current and the lake.

But I think a truer image is the whirlpools of the current itself, occurring and recurring, the same? or not the same?

I worked at the mathematics of an explanation in the early years of my marriage, while my physics was still in good working order. See the "Notes toward a Theory of Resonance Interference in Doubled Ansible and Churten Fields," appended to this document. I realize that the explanation is probably irrelevant, since, on this stretch of the river, there is no Tiokunan'n Field. But independent research from an odd direction can be useful. And I am attached to it, since it is the last temporal physics I did. I have followed churten research with intense interest, but my life's work has been concerned with vineyards, drainage, the care of yamas, the care and education of children, the Discussions, and trying to learn how to catch fish with my bare hands.

Working on that paper, I satisfied myself in terms of mathematics and physics that the existence in which I went to Hain and became a temporal physicist specializing in transilience was in fact encapsulated (enfolded, erased) by the churten effect. But no amount of theory or proof could quite allay my anxiety, my fear—which increased after my marriage and with the birth of each of my children—that there was a crossing point yet to come. For all my images of rivers and whirlpools, I could not prove that the encapsulation might not reverse at the instant of transilience. It was possible that on the day I churtened from Ve to Ran'n I might undo, lose, erase my marriage, our children, all my life at Udan, crumple it up like a bit of paper tossed into a basket. I could not endure that thought.

I spoke of it at last to Isidri, from whom I have only ever kept one secret.

"No," she said, after thinking a long time, "I don't think that can be. There was a reason, wasn't there, that you came back—here."

"You," I said.

She smiled wonderfully. "Yes," she said. She added after a while, "And Sota, and Koneko, and the farmhold . . . But there'd be no reason for you to go back there, would there?"

She was holding our sleeping baby as she spoke; she laid her cheek against the small silky head.

"Except maybe your work there," she said. She looked at me with a little yearning in her eyes. Her honesty required equal honesty of me.

"I miss it sometimes," I said. "I know that. I didn't know that I was missing you. But I was dying of it. I would have died and never known why, Isidri. And anyhow, it was all wrong—my work was wrong."

•

"How could it have been wrong, if it brought you back?" she said, and to that I had no answer at all.

When information on churten theory began to be published I subscribed to whatever the Center Library of O received, particularly the work done at the Ekumenical Schools and on Ve. The general progress of research was just as I remembered, racing along for three years, then hitting the hard places. But there was no reference to a Tiokunan'n Hideo doing research in the field. Nobody worked on a theory of a stabilized double field. No churten field research station was set up at Ran'n.

At last it was the winter of my visit home, and then the very day; and I will admit that, all reason to the contrary, it was a bad day. I felt waves of guilt, of nausea. I grew very shaky, thinking of the Udan of that visit, when Isidri had been married to Hedran, and I a mere visitor.

Hedran, a respected traveling scholar of the Discussions, had in fact come to teach several times in the village. Isidri had suggested inviting him to stay at Udan. I had vetoed the suggestion, saying that though he was a brilliant teacher there was something I disliked about him. I got a sidelong flash from Sidi's clear dark eyes: *Is he jealous?* She suppressed a smile. When I told her and my mother about my "other life," the one thing I had left out, the one secret I kept, was my visit to Udan. I did not want to tell my mother that in that "other life" she had been very ill. I did not want to tell Isidri that in that "other life" Hedran had been her Evening husband and she had had no children of her body. Perhaps I was wrong, but it seemed to me that I had no right to tell these things, that they were not mine to tell.

So Isidri could not know that what I felt was less jealousy than guilt. I had kept knowledge from her.

And I had deprived Hedran of a life with Isidri, the dear joy, the center, the life of my own life.

Or had I shared it with him? I didn't know. I don't know.

That day passed like any other, except that one of Suudi's children broke her elbow falling out of a tree. "At least we know she won't drown," said Tubdu, wheezing.

Next came the date of the night in my rooms in the New Quadrangle, when I had wept and not known why I wept. And a while after that, the day of my return, transilient, to Ve, carrying a bottle of Isidri's wine for Gvonesh. And finally, yesterday, I entered the churten field on Ve, and left it eighteen years ago on O. I spent the night, as I sometimes do, in the shrine. The hours went by quietly; I wrote, gave worship, meditated, and slept. And I woke beside the pool of silent water.

So, now: I hope the Stabiles will accept this report from a farmer they never heard of, and that the engineers of transilience may see it as at least a footnote to their experiments. Certainly it is difficult to verify, the only evidence for it being my word, and my otherwise almost inexplicable knowledge of churten theory. To Gvonesh, who does not know me, I send my respect, my gratitude, and my hope that she will honor my intent.

◼ HarperPrism

A Fisherman of the Inland Sea
by Ursula K. Le Guin

The National Book Award-winning author's new collection has all the majesty and appeal of her major works. Here we have starships that sail, literally, on wings of song . . . musical instruments to be played at funerals only. . . *ansibles*, faster-than-light communication . . . orbiting arks designed to save a doomed humanity.

Also by Ursula K. Le Guin

Searoad: Chronicles of Klatsand
Here is the culmination of Le Guin's lifelong fascination with small island cultures. In a sense, the Klatsand of these stories is a modern world apart from our own, but part of it as well.

The Dispossessed
A brilliant physicist makes an unprecedented journey to the utopian mother planet to challenge the complex structures of life and living, and ignite the fires of change.

The Beginning Place
Two young people meet in a strange and wonderful place across the creek and escape from their dreary daily lives. But when their place of peace becomes a realm of horror, they suddenly face a terrible and chilling choice that could cost them everything, including their lives.

The Eye of the Heron
The People of the Peace are brutalized and dominated by the City criminals. They would have broken vows and shed blood if not for one bold young woman who leaves her City father to lead the People on a perilous quest to discover a world of hope within this world of chaos . . . a place they will call Heron.

The Compass Rose

Twenty astonishing stories that carry us to worlds of wonder and horror, desire and destiny, enchantment and doom.

Orsinian Tales

In this enchanting collection, Ursula K. Le Guin brings to mainstream fiction the same compelling mastery of word and deed, of story and character, of violence and love, that has won the Hugo, the Nebula, and the National Book Awards.